How Far Are You Willing To Go?
Murder Is Just The Beginning
(Rated PG) Part 3

How Far Are You Willing To Go?
Murder Is Just The Beginning
(Rated PG) Part 3

BY

TRACY WILSON

http://beautifulpublications.com

Published by
Beautiful Publications LLC
Stratford, CT 06614

This book is a work of fiction. Names, characters, places, and incidents are either products of the author's imagination or are used fictitiously. Any resemblance to actual events or locales or persons, living or dead, is entirely coincidental.

©Copyright 2017 Tracy Wilson

PRINT ISBN: 978-0-9985765-2-7
EBOOK ISBN: 978-0-9985765-5-8

Printed in the United States of America

Dedication

This series is dedicated to my granddaughter, Shaliyah.

Chapter 83

When we got there, my mother and my grandmother were waiting for us.

"Shit!" I said out loud.

"What's wrong Trenice?"

"I can't tell you Char – not yet anyway..."

"Well when can you tell me?"

"After they leave."

"Ok – but I'm still comin' upstairs..."

"Ok."

"Hi Miss Claire, hi Miss Gladys." Jordan said.

"Hi Jordan. Y'all just leavin' the hospital?"

"Yea Grandma."

"We wanna talk to you Trenice."

1

"I kinda figured that Ma," I said as we all followed Jordan into the house.

"Damn – what the hell is that smell?" Char yelled.

"That's coming from where I threw up in the kitchen."

"Oh so that's why you were in the hospital?"

"Yea."

"Well damn Trenice – how much did you drink?"

"I drank ½ gallon of Bacardi 151."

"You drank ½ gallon of 151?"

"Yup."

"Oh my God – why Trenice?"

"That's why we're here Char," my mother said.

"Jordan said he was going to Shoprite."

"Yea? So?" Grandma asked as she inched closer to me. I swear – I didn't know if she wanted to hug me or knock the shit out of me...

"So he said he'd be right back."

"So what happened Trenice?" my mother asked.

"I sat down here in the living room to watch television. I started flickin' the channels like I always do and there was nothing on, so I turned on News 12."

"I don't understand Trenice," my mother said.

"What's News 12 got to do with what happened?"

"Have you seen News 12 Ma?"

"No Trenice."

"Thomas Johnson is dead."

"What?" they said in unison.

"He's dead. My father's dead," I said with tears in my eyes.

"Oh my God – you poor child," Grandma said as she hugged me. "Did you tell Trudy?" my mother asked.

"I didn't tell anybody until just now. I'm still tryin' to deal with the fact that Trudy's my sister."

"Your sister?" We all forgot Char was sitting there.

"Yea – Trudy's my sister."

"I thought she was your Aunt?"

"She is my Aunt. She's my Aunt and my sister."

"Oh God – I'm gettin' a headache..." Char said.

"Well don't look for any Tylenol – I tried that already..." I said.

"You mean you really were tryin' to kill yourself?"

"To be honest Ma – I don't know what I was tryin' to do. After I saw News 12 all I wanted to do was stop the pain. I ran into the bathroom and looked for the bottle of Tylenol. I got mad when it was empty so I threw it. I went in the kitchen, opened the bottle of Bacardi, and started drinkin'... I kept drinkin' until I was numb. I tried to get up and go to the bathroom but I slid back down onto the floor. Next thing I know, I'm looking down at myself laying in my own vomit mixed with blood.

"What do you mean looking down at yourself?" Char asked.

"I left my body Char. I thought I was dead," I said as I started to cry."

"Oh my God Trenice – why didn't you call me?" she said as we hugged each other and cried.

"I tried to call you when I first saw the news but your line was busy. I didn't think to call anybody else - I just wanted to stop the pain," I said as I continued to cry.

"I was comin' back Trenice," Jordan said as he started to cry too.

"I'm sorry," I said as we hugged each other and cried.

"Oh my God – stop it!" Char yelled.

"Can't stand to see a man cry eh?" Jordan laughed.

"I can't stop cryin' Char – it hurts too much."

"I'm here baby – I'm here," Jordan said as he held me and let me cry.

"I never should've told you Trenice," my mother said.

"I was gonna find out sooner or later anyway Ma."

"You're probably right Trenice."

"You alright Miss Gladys?" Jordan asked.

"Not really – I'll be ok – I just need to make sure Trenice is ok."

"She'll be alright – I'll see to it…"

"I know you will Jordan. C'mon Claire – let's go."

"Wait!" I yelled so loud I startled all of them. "Sit down!"

"Who you talkin' too Trenice?"

"You Grandma – sit down!"

"Girl don't le'me…"

"Dammit Grandma – shut up and sit down!"

"Ok Trenice. We're sitting down. Now what's wrong?"

"Thomas Johnson was my father."

"We know that Trenice," my mother said.

"Ma shut up!"

Jordan and Char looked at me in shock. They both sat there without saying a word.

"What is it Trenice?" Grandma asked as she took my hand. "What's wrong?"

"Thomas was my father. Thomas was Trudy's father. Thomas was also Cornell's father."

No one said anything.

"Did you hear what I said?"

"Yea Trenice, we heard you. C'mon Claire let's go."

"Wait a minute Ma."

"Now Claire."

"No Ma. We need to hear this."

"I don't need to hear anymore," Grandma said as she started to cry."

"Oh yes you do too – and so do I - go ahead Trenice," my mother said.

"Why you cryin' Miss Gladys? Y'all makin' me cry," Char said as she started crying again.

"Char le'me finish..." I said.

"Ok."

"Remember the explosion at the gas station?"

"Yea, I remember."

"News 12 said the 2nd body was identified as Thomas Johnson."

"So how you know Thomas Johnson was Cornell's father too?"

"News 12 said so. They were in jail together and they were paroled at the same time."

"This is unfuckin' believable!" Grandma yelled.

"You ok Ma?" my mother asked.

"Hell no ...far from it..."

"I can't believe that monster was your brother," Jordan said.

"And Trudy's brother..." Grandma said.

"And Tony's brother..." I said.

"We might as well go now Claire," Grandma said as she stood up. "I've had enough of this shit."

"Have you Grandma?"

"Trenice!" Jordan yelled.

"Well? Have you had enough Grandma?" I don't remember leaving the couch but I remember hitting the floor...

"Bitch, don't you ever..."

"Ma – leave her alone!" my mother yelled.

"Figures," I said as I picked myself up off the floor... "You just don't get it do you Grandma? Truth hurts doesn't it?"

"That's enough Trenice...."

"Like hell it is! I'm not the one that fucked your man – she is!" I screamed.

"Alright everybody get the fuck out!" Jordan yelled.

"No, no, no, no, no!" I screamed. "They wanna know what the fuck is wrong so I'm gonna tell 'em!"

"Trenice that's not fair!" my mother cried. "We were trying to protect you! We had your best interest at heart!"

"Oh yea? Who were you tryin' to protect when you told Aunt Trudy?"

"Trudy? What the hell are you talkin' about Trenice?"

"Tell her Grandma – go ahead and tell her..."

"Ma! You told Trudy?"

"Yea – I told Trudy – so what?"

"And you wonder why she's always goin' after Trenice? What the hell were you thinkin' Ma?"

"Oh Ma don't act so shocked – you told Miss April and Miss June."

"Claire! What the hell were you thinkin'?"

"I wasn't thinking' at all and neither were you – isn't that right Ma?"

"Bitch I'll knock the shit outta you..."

"No you won't either Grandma," I said.

"What the fuck did you say to me?"

"I said you're not gonna hit my mother. And you're not gonna hit me again either."

We all sat there and watched as Grandma got up, left, and slammed the door behind her so hard the wall unit and everything in it started to shake.

"I'm sorry Trenice. I wish I never met that man – I'm glad the son-of-a-bitch is dead!" my mother yelled.

"Who you tellin'?" I laughed.

"You ok Char? Char? Earth to Char?"

"Trenice you got anything to drink?"

"Yea Char – why?"

"Cause I need a strong one."

"Make that two," my mother said.

"Trenice you want one?"

"Honey I don't want anything stronger than coffee," I laughed.

"Ok – I'll be back in a few..." Jordan said as he got up to go in the kitchen.

"Miss Claire?"

"Yes Char?"

"I'm not tryin' to be all up in your business, but..."

"And we wasn't tryin' to be all up in yours but we all up in it anyway ain't we?"

"You have a point," Char laughed.

"I thought we told you we wanted a strong drink?" Char said as Jordan handed us all a cup of coffee.

"Black coffee – no sugar – no cream – pretty strong to me," Jordan laughed.

"Besides – after what Trenice has been through – the last thing we need to be drinkin' is liquor," Jordan said as he sat down next to me.

"You ok Trenice?"

"Yea. It felt good to let that out."

"I had no idea you were so angry Trenice. Can you forgive me?"

"Of course I can forgive you Ma. I just can't forget it."

"I can't either Trenice. I wish I could."

"You don't understand how I feel Ma."

"I think I do Trenice."

"No you don't. Everybody knew but me. You knew. Grandma knew. Miss April new. Miss June new. Aunt Trudy knew. I feel like I was the butt of a joke. I feel like I'm a piece of garbage. I feel like everybody looks at me as an ugly secret. I feel like everyone looks at me and all they see is incest. I'm the black sheep in this family. You know what Trudy said before I woke up in the hospital Ma?"

"What Trenice?"

"She said she wonder if I got drunk 'cause I know she's my sister?"

"Oh my God Trenice – I'm sorry!"

"Why did Grandma have to tell her Ma? Why did you have to tell anybody? Why was I even born?" I cried.

"Stop it!" Jordan cried. You were born for me!"

"And me!" Char cried.

"Trenice I love you. I wanted you. That's why you were born."

"Why'd you do it Ma?"

"Trenice I didn't know – I swear – I didn't know."

"You didn't know Ma?"

"No Trenice. I thought Trudy and I had the same father. I didn't find out you and Trudy had the same father until after you were born."

"Really?"

"Yes, Trenice. After you were born Ma started askin' questions about your father. I didn't think anything of it until she told me you and Trudy have the same birthmark."

"Damn – it's not enough she's my Aunt and my sister – we gotta have the same birthmark too?"

"Yes."

"So how did you…"

"I met Thomas at the 'Blue Flame' on Ravine Avenue before he went to prison. He introduced himself, we had a few drinks, one thing led to another, we went back to his place, and we hit it off. Neil and I never stopped seeing each other so when I got pregnant, I never thought Thomas was your father. He went to prison right after you were born so I figured we'd never have to worry about it. I never would've got involved with him if I knew he'd been with my mother. "

"Damn Ma – I'm sorry."

"You have nothing to be sorry for Trenice."

"Damn – I was fuckin' your brother," Char laughed. "Cornell was your brother...Tony's your brother...and Sissy is your sister-in-law."

"Yea – and Trudy too Char."

"Damn Trenice – Sissy is Trudy's sister in law and your sister-in-law."

"I know Char...Oh my God!"

"What Trenice?" my mother asked.

"I almost fucked my brother!" I laughed.

"What?" they all yelled in unison.

"Not Cornell!"

"Whew girl – don't scare me like that!" Char yelled."

"Who Trenice?" my mother asked.

"Tony."

"Then Damn!" Char yelled.

"Trenice please tell me you didn't..." my mother said.

11

"No Ma. Not even close. Not even so much as a kiss. All we said was hi and bye."

"Oh thank God!"

"We'll probably say more than that now..." I said.

"Why you gotta talk to him Trenice? You don't have to say a fuckin' thing to him!" Jordan yelled.

"He's my brother, Jordan."

"Don't fuckin' remind me," Jordan mumbled.

"Honey – all I'm saying is you know Gramdna gonna tell Aunt Trudy. Aunt Trudy probably gonna tell Sissy. They gonna see it on News 12. Everybody will know.

"You probably right Trenice," my mother said.

"Trenice?"

"Yea Char?"

"How you find out you and Trudy had the same father?"

"Miss June told me when she was drunk."

"That bitch!" my mother yelled.

"Ma! That's Jordan's mother!"

"Yea and she's also my friend – that bitch!"

"Ma – forget it."

"Forget it? Can you forget it Trenice?"

"Ma – that's like me bein' mad at Aunt Trudy 'cause she knew all this time – which I am mind you – but what's the point?"

"You're right Trenice...well I might as well go home. I'll see you soon."

"You think Grandma will ever speak to us again Ma?"

"Eventually. But I do think you owe her an apology though."

"No I don't either. I know I'm your baby 'n all but I'm also a grown woman. I have a right to my feelings and this is my house."

"Ok Trenice – calm down."

"I am calm Ma. I'm just saying no one really has a right to be mad at me for anything..."

"You're right Trenice," Jordan said.

"That's your grandmother Trenice. She took care of you."

"I know who she is Ma. The problem is I'm still tryin' to figure out who the hell I am."

"Good bye Trenice," my mother said as she slammed the door.

"What the fuck is their problem? How the fuck they gonna get mad at you?" Char asked.

"Who gives a damn – let 'em stay mad!" Jordan yelled. "I'm sick of this shit! Only reason you didn't get thrown out is 'cause Trenice wouldn't let me throw you out!" Jordan yelled.

"It was time they knew how I felt, Jordan. I should'a let them know as soon as they told me. Instead I turned it all inside and let it eat at me. Then, when I couldn't take it anymore, I turned to Bacardi 'cause I felt like there wasn't anything or anybody else I could turn to."

13

"You didn't have to do that Trenice...I was on my way back..."

"You weren't here. You don't know how I was feeling..."

"Why was I gettin' thrown out?" We'd forgotten Char was sitting there.

"What?" we said in unison.

"Jordan wanted to throw me out."

"I didn't want to throw you out Char." Jordan said. "I wanted everyone to get out. I was sick of seeing Trenice hurting. I was sick of hearing her cry. Then her grandmother had the nerve to start cryin'. I'd had enough."

"So you not throwin' me out?" Char asked.

"Girl, shut up!" we both yelled in unison.

"Y'all are crazy," Char laughed.

"I'ma go clean the kitchen while you talk to Char," Jordan said.

"Trenice?"

"Yea Char?"

"Cornell raped you didn't he?"

"Yea Char."

"I thought so."

"I'm glad you didn't ask me that in front of my mother and grandmother.

"I almost did when you said you almost fucked your brother."

"Thank God you didn't."

"I'm surprised you didn't tell your mother."

"I can't ever tell her Char."

"Why Trenice?"

"You have to ask?"

"I see your point."

"I can't tell anyone else."

"Who else knows?"

"Jordan."

"And?"

"Dr. Campana."

"And?"

"Dr. Campton."

"And?"

"Jake and Rachel."

"Why you tell them?"

"Jake is Jordan's best friend."

"Why you tell Rachel?"

"That's his wife."

"You could'a told me too Trenice."

"No I couldn't."

"Why not?"

"You don't understand Char."

"So make me understand then."

"Remember when I went to get my cast off?"

"Yea."

"Jordan and I had sex before I left..."

"When don't you have sex Trenice..."

"Le'me finish..."

"Ok."

"I was so happy I went to the Food Emporium to buy dinner."

"Why didn't you come home and go to Shoprite?"

"Char!"

"Sorry – go 'head."

"I called a cab so when Cornell pulled up..."

"Cornell?"

"Yea."

"I thought you said he didn't take you home?"

"He didn't."

"Ok – go 'head."

"He asked if I called a cab so I got in..."

"Ok."

"He said he had to stop at his garage and he would just be a few minutes..."

"Oh my God..."

"I figured since he was doing whatever he was doing I would go to the bathroom..."

"Oh my God..."

"He came in there and put a knife to my throat..."

"Oh my God, Oh my God, Oh my God..."

"When he was finished he turned his back to fix his clothes..."

"Why you stop Trenice?" I didn't answer her. "Trenice what happened?"

"I picked up the cover off the back of the toilet..."

"Oh my God..."

"I hit him over and over again until it broke into little pieces."

"Then?"

"He died." Char sat there for a few minutes without saying anything.

"Oh my God – you killed him!" Char screamed.

"Yea Char. I killed my brother. He raped me and I killed him."

"It all makes sense. All those questions. Everything they said. Everything you said. It all makes sense."

"I was praying I was wrong Char. I wanted it to be someone else... anybody else... especially after I found out I was pregnant..."

"Oh my God Trenice – you really didn't know whose baby it was..."

"No Char. I had so much going on and no one to talk too...I was scared to death Char... scared I had aids...scared Jordan had aids...scared you had aids... hell – I was even scared Sissy had aids."

"Oh my God Trenice! You tried to make me think it was drug related!"

"I had no choice Char! Once I saw News 12 I had no choice. All I could think about was what if I was carrying that monster's child... what if my baby and Sissy's baby looked alike?"

"Oh my God – I forgot about that!"

"That's why I was askin' you all those questions. Once you told me you were tryin' to have his baby I knew Sissy wasn't pregnant by Cornell and neither was I."

"Oh my God – you lost Jordan's baby!"

"Yea Char...I lost our baby."

"Were you ever gonna tell me Trenice?"

"Yea."

"For real?"

"Yea – they wanted me to tell you sooner."

"They?"

"Yea – Jordan, Jake, and Rachel."

"Oh... Trenice?"

"Yea Char?"

"Do they know you killed him?"

"Yea."

"Does anybody else know you killed him?"

"Yea."

"Who?"

"Dr. Campton."

"Anybody else?"

"Yea."

"Who?"

"His nurse."

"Oh... Trenice?"

"Yea Char?"

"Did you tell the police?"

"No."

"Why?"

"I didn't think they'd believe me."

"Oh... Why you tell the nurse?"

"I didn't."

"How she find out?"

"She overheard me talkin' to the doctor."

"How you know she won't tell nobody?"

"Cause she's glad I killed him."

"Why?"

"Cause he raped her too."

"Then Damn!"

"Char?"

"Yea Trenice?"

"I wish you were married to Cornell instead of Sissy."

"Why you say that?"

"Cause you would've been my sister-in-law and my best friend."

"And my husband would have been a monster."

"No he wouldn't have."

"What makes you say that?"

"Cause he never hurt you."

"But he hurt you Trenice. And he hurt other people."

"If you married him you would've introduced him to me. He would've found out I was in love with his buddy from high school. Then, later on he would've found out he was my brother and I was his sister. We would've been one happy family."

"I doubt it Trenice."

"I doubt it too," Jordan said as he walked into the living room.

"Trenice?"

"Yea Char?"

"You got drunk 'cause you was tryin' to stop the pain right?"

"Yea Char."

"You didn't give a damn about Thomas being your father. You couldn't deal with the fact that you were raped by your own brother."

"Char when I saw News 12 it was like he raped me all over again on top of all this other shit."

"Your mother, your grandmother, and Trudy don't have a fuckin' clue."

"And they never will Char. You and Jordan are the only ones that know I was raped by my brother."

"No we're not." Jordan said.

"Who else knows?" Char asked.

"We told Jake and Rachel, Trenice."

"We told them I was raped. We never told them Cornell was my brother."

"No we didn't. But once they find out Thomas Johnson was your father, they'll know," Jordan said.

"Who's gonna tell them?" I asked.

"I hope nobody ever tells them Trenice. I hope nobody ever tells them," Jordan said.

"Trenice?"

"Yea Char?"

"Do you know what happened to your father?"

"News 12 thinks Cornell killed him."

"That's not what I asked you."

"No Char – I don't know what happened to Thomas Johnson."

"Did you have anything to do with the explosion?"

"No Char."

"I still think you could'a told me."

"I know."

"Well I might as well go home."

"You aiight Char?" Jordan asked.

"Not really. But I will be. I can definitely move on now."

"Glad to hear it Char."

"My friend's supposed to be comin' to pick me up in a few hours…"

"Your friend?" we said in unison.

"Oh I forgot…I haven't talked to you in a while…yea, I got me a new friend girl!"

"And you thought you were leavin'? Girl, sit your ass down!" I laughed as I pushed her back down onto the couch.

Jordan smiled to himself as he watched us laughing and talking like old times. "Thank you Lord," he said as he went into the bedroom.

Chapter 84

"We interrupt our regularly scheduled programming to bring you this latest bulletin from News 12. Dr. Aiden has been arrested and charged with attempted rape. According to the Yonkers Police, charges were brought against Dr. Aiden after a patient in the E.R. gave a statement, which was later corroborated by security footage provided by St. Joseph's Hospital. Dr. Aiden has been fired from St. Joseph's Hospital effective immediately. We now continue with our regularly scheduled programming..."

Chapter 85

"Where's Char?" I yawned.

"She went home after you fell asleep.

"How long have I been asleep? What time is it?"

"It's 6:00 p.m."

"Damn! I been asleep all afternoon? Why didn't you wake me up?"

"For what?"

"So I could come to bed," I whispered in his ear as I snuggled up next to him.

"Welcome back Beautiful," he said as he pulled me into a kiss..."

"Someone's at the door..." I said as I began kissing his neck...

"Fuck 'em – they'll go away..." he said as he nibbled on my earlobe..."

"It could be important..." I said.

"This is important..." he said.

"Jordan! You in there?"

"Hold on..." Jordan yelled as he jumped up to answer the door.

"Hey guys," I said as Jake and Rachel walked into the living room.

"Y'all up for company?" Jake asked. Jordan just laughed and shook his head...

"Oh boy – we better sit down," Rachel said as she plopped down on the couch beside me.

"So what brings you here?" Jordan asked. Neither one of them spoke.

"Honey?"

"Yea?"

"I'm starving!"

"I forgot you haven't eaten in two days," he laughed.

"I guess you would be starving – why haven't you eaten in two days?"

"Long story Rachel – long, long story."

"Well we got nothin' but time," Rachel laughed as she pulled off her shoes and stretched back on the couch.

"What can I get ya Beautiful?"

"Scrambled eggs 'n cheddar cheese with peppers, onions, and garlic, turkey sausage, buttermilk biscuits, home fries, and kiwi lemonade – and that's just for breakfast – for dinner I want spaghetti with meatballs, sweet Italian sausage, onions, peppers, and mushrooms."

"You don't want much do you?" he laughed.

"She did say she was hungry man," Jake laughed.

"Let's do this," Jordan said as he pulled Jake by the arm.

"I love a man that cooks," Rachel laughed.

"Amen!" I laughed.

"Maybe we should go in the kitchen and see if they need any help..."

"Naaa...." We laughed in unison. We sat there watching the channels go from one to the other to the other as Rachel flicked the remote.

"Damn – nothing on TV," Rachel said.

"Thank God," I mumbled.

"Watchu say?"

"Nothin'," I said as I got up to turn on the stereo.

"Sounds good to me...Ohh shit – that's my song!" Rachel yelled as we started dancing to 'Betchall Never Find.'

"Go ladies – it's your birthday – it's your birthday," Jake said as they started dancing with us.

"Aww shit...they playin' the extended version!" I yelled as we kept on dancing.

"Damn that food smells good – y'all ready to eat?"

"I am," Rachel laughed.

"Trenice hasn't had a good meal in two days – you had breakfast and lunch!" Jake laughed.

"And your point is?"

We all bust out laughing.

"I believe the question was, are y'all ready to eat – not when's the last time y'all ate," I laughed.

"Tell 'em Trenice," Rachel laughed.

"I'm about to show 'em girl!" I laughed as I grabbed Rachel's hand and we headed to the dining room with Jordan and Jake behind us.

"Look at 'em man – not even so much as a thank you," Jake laughed. I stopped in the doorway, turned around, and put my hands on my hips.

"Uh oh...," Jordan said.

"Trenice, I was only kidding," Jake said.

"Maybe you were kidding but I'm not," I said as I pulled Jake and Rachel into a hug.

"What's wrong Trenice?" Jake asked when he saw tears in my eyes.

"Nothing."

"You sure?"

"I'm sure," I said as Jake tried to pull away from me and I snatched him back into the hug with me and Rachel.

"You sure you ok Trenice?" Rachel asked.

"I'm gettin' there."

"Can we eat now?" Jordan asked.

"Not yet...I'm not done..."

"Okay then," Jordan laughed.

"Thank you for breakfast, for being our friends, and for being there when we need you," I said.

"Awww... you're welcome," they said as they hugged me back.

"Le'me get somadat," Jordan said as he pushed his way in and we all hugged each other.

"Now can we eat Trenice?"

"Not yet sweetie."

"Ooookkaaaayy...," Jordan sighed as we all stopped hugging each other.

"Thank you for loving me unconditionally and seeing my beauty – even when I don't," I said as I pulled Jordan into a deep kiss.

"You're welcome," he said as he kissed me back for a few minutes...

"Oh – sorry – I guess y'all hungry – c'mon, Jordan," I said as I took him by the hand and went through the doorway into the dining room.

"Now that's the Trenice we know and love," Jake said as we all sat down at the table.

"I'm happy to see you two so happy but I know some shit went down in here...I can feel it."

"You're right Rachel."

"So you gonna tell us what happened or do I have to make you tell us?"

"I don't have the energy to keep you from tickling me Rachel so let's just eat – but I have to do one more thing before we eat..."

"Ok Trenice – go 'head."

"Can we all hold hands?" I asked.

"Ok," Jordan said as he took Rachel and Jake's hands on the right side of the table and I took Jake and Rachel's hands on the left side of the table.

"Dear Lord, thank you for this food. Thank you for sending us such wonderful husbands. Thank you for showing me that I am not alone in this world and for being there with me when no one else could hear me. Thank you for bringing me back. Amen."

"Amen!" they all said in unison.

"Trenice?"

"Yea Rachel?"

"What did you mean by that?"

"Let's eat Rachel," I said.

"Ok."

Jordan and Jake looked at each other without saying a word. Rachel looked at me and I looked back at her, but we all continued eating without talking, except for the usual – "pass the ketchup, pass the salt & pepper, pass the biscuits, more coffee, more lemonade?" etc., until we were stuffed.

"I'm not ready to eat again yet, but that spaghetti sauce sure smells good," I said.

"We'll let it simmer while we go back in the living room" Jordan said as he put his arm around my waist, pulled me close to him, and we all walked back into the living room.

"Give me that!" I said as I snatched the remote from Rachel.

"All you had to do was say you didn't wanna watch TV Trenice – damn!"

"I'm sorry Rachel – it's just that I've had enough TV for today."

"I bet," Jake said.

"Whatchu mean by that man?" Jordan asked.

"Dammit Jake!" Rachel yelled.

"What?" Jake asked.

"I thought you said we weren't gonna tell 'em!" Rachel said.

"Tell us what?" Jordan asked.

"We saw News 12," Rachel said.

"Oh...so I guess you know everything then," I said.

"Yea, Trenice – we know."

"We came over to see if you were alright," Jake said.

"I just got home from the hospital earlier today."

"Oh my God! – You alright?"

"Yea. That's what I meant when I said 'Thank you for bringing me back.'"

"Trenice – don't tell me – you almost died?" Rachel asked with tears in her eyes.

"Yea."

"What happened Trenice?"

"Jordan wasn't here when I saw News 12, so I got the ½ gallon of Bacardi 151 and drank until I was numb."

"Oh my God! You drank the whole thing?"

"Yea...next thing I knew I was looking down at myself lying in my own vomit mixed with blood."

"Damn man – musta been hard seeing Trenice like that." Jake said as he put his hand on Jordan's shoulder.

"I've never seen anything like that in my life...and I don't ever wanna see anything like that ever again..."

"Im sorry honey..."

"I know baby – I know..."

"You were looking down at yourself Trenice? You mean you left your body?" Rachel asked.

"Yea."

"Wow!"

"I saw everything. I saw when Jordan found me. I saw when they put me in the ambulance. Every time I cried, Jordan could hear me."

"Huh?" they said in unison.

"She was crying 'cause she wanted to wake up but she couldn't," Jordan said.

"Oh my God – I've heard about people being connected but I've never actually met anyone that it actually happened too...Wow!"

"I'm surprised myself, Rachel."

"That's some shit, man," Jake said.

"Her Aunt Trudy thought I was crazy," Jordan laughed.

"Figures," Jake laughed.

"Miss Gladys set 'em straight though."

"She did?"

"Yea...she reminded them how she heard them when she had her heart attack last year."

"She did?" Rachel asked.

"Yea. She even helped my mother find her wallet," I laughed.

"Oh she told you Trenice?"

"No – I saw them and heard them talking up until the time I woke up."

"Wow – I can't believe this shit!" Rachel yelled.

"I saw Jordan turn on News 12 and watched it. That's when he found out..."

"Damn man – I'm sorry," Jake said.

"I had no idea Trenice..." Jordan said.

"I know..."

"I wish I was here with you..."

"I know...I wish you were here too..."

"Well, he's here now Trenice," Jake said.

"I know...he's always been here...it's just that..."

"I can't imagine what you were going through Trenice," Rachel said.

"I could've dealt with me and Trudy having the same father as long as he stayed away...but nooo...he had to get released...he had to come back here...then I had to find out I was raped by my own brother...that was the last straw..."

"I wonder why he came back here?" Rachel asked, interrupting my thoughts...

"Who the hell knows?" Jordan said.

"You think Cornell killed him?" Jake asked.

"I have no idea – probably."

"Char asked Trenice if she did it," Jordan said.

"Get the fuck outta here! – When?"

"Today."

"Hold up – Char was here?"

"Yea – and she wasn't the only one," Jordan said.

"What the fuck went on here?" Jake asked.

"All hell broke loose man – all hell broke loose!" Jordan said.

"Oh my God – what happened Trenice?"

"Everything Rachel."

"I'm confused."

"I'll start at the beginning."

"Please."

"We were leaving the hospital and we ran into Char."

"Oh boy...I bet that didn't go over too well," Jake said.

"Actually, I was happy to see her until she told me she was at the hospital to get her test results."

"Oh my God! – Is she okay?"

"Yea Rachel – we're fine." Rachel sat there for a few seconds...

"Oh! I got it!"

"'Bout time," Jake laughed.

"Trenice invited Char back here to tell her everything but when we got here, Miss Gladys and Miss Claire were here waiting for us," Jordan said.

"Damn!" Jake yelled.

"I let them have it Rachel...I told them exactly how I felt."

"You did? How'd they take it?"

"Miss Gladys knocked the shit outta Trenice," Jordan laughed.

"Get the fuck outta here! Why?"

"Well Rachel, she said she had enough of this shit and she tried to leave, so I asked her if she was sure...next thing you know, I'm picking myself up off the floor."

"Oh my God!"

"Oh it gets even better...I told her I'm not the one that fucked your man – she is!"

"Jordan was here when you said that shit?"

"Yea I was here – I told them get the fuck out but Trenice said no – they wanna know what the fuck is wrong so she gonna fuckin' tell 'em!" Jordan yelled.

"You go girl!" Rachel yelled as she gave me a high 5.

"And Miss Gladys cryin' 'n shit 'cause she didn't wanna hear it – but she wasn't cryin' when she knocked the shit outta Trenice though."

"I bet she was mad as hell too," Rachel said.

"You should'a seen the look on her face when Trenice told her she wasn't gonna hit her again..."

"You did what? Damn girl!"

"I had to Rachel. I was telling them about News 12. My grandmother started cryin' at first 'cause it was bringing up old memories. My mother made her stay so I could finish telling them – but she knocked the shit outta me 'cause I was throwing it back up in her face 'cause she told Aunt Trudy."

"Damn!" they said in unison.

"My mother didn't know Aunt Trudy knew so she got mad too. That's when my grandmother said she would knock the shit outta her."

"Did she?"

"No Rachel. I told her you're not gonna hit my mother and you're not gonna hit me again either."

"Where was Char all this time?"

"Right there," I said.

"Wow! So what'd she do?" Rachel asked.

"She let the doorknob hit her in the ass," Jordan laughed.

"Man, you gotta be shittin' me," Jake laughed.

"I'm serious. Then when Miss Claire tried to tell Trenice she owed Miss Gladys an apology, Trenice told her she didn't owe her shit – she a grown woman and this is her house!"

"Girl, I never knew you had it in you!" Rachel yelled.

"That's the problem Rachel – it was in me for too long and I ended up turning it inward."

"Damn – sorry Trenice."

"Miss Claire let the doorknob hit her in the ass too," Jordan laughed.

"They got a lot a shit with them don't they?" Jake said.

"They sure do...only reason they stayed as long as they did was 'cause of Trenice. I got tired of her hurtin' and cryin' 'cause of them."

"I hear you man – but Trenice was right – they needed to hear it – whether they liked it or not," Jake said.

"So what did Char have to say about all this?"

"She nearly fell outta her chair when Trenice said she wished Char married Cornell instead of Sissy," Jordan said.

"Why Trenice?" Rachel asked.

"Rachel, if Char married Cornell, she would've been my sister-in-law and my best friend... Cornell would've found out I was his sister... they would've all been on the court just like the good ole days...we would've been happy..."

35

"You really think so Trenice?"

"Probably."

"So did you get a chance to tell Char everything?"

"Yea."

"How she take it?"

"Better than I thought."

"Really?"

"Yea – she still thinks I could'a told her – especially 'cause y'all know."

"Damn – you told her all that?"

"Yes I did. I told her all of it. And I'm glad I did."

"You think she's gonna be ok?"

"Oh please – she already has another friend," Jordan laughed.

"Yea, she'll be fine alright," Rachel laughed.

"Trenice?"

"Yea Rachel?"

"You didn't tell your mother or your grandmother about Cornell did you?"

"Hell no – and I never will."

"I wouldn't either!" Jake yelled.

"But Char knows, right?"

"Yes Rachel...Char knows I was raped by my own brother."

"Wait a minute!" Jake yelled...

"What's wrong man?" Jordan asked.

"Cornell was your brother, so he's Trudy's brother too right?"

"Yea... and Tony's brother," Jordan said.

"Tony? The one Trenice was talking too?"

"Yea."

"Wow...next thing you know – we'll all be cousins," Jake laughed.

"That's a whole other chapter," Jordan laughed as we followed him into the dining room, sat down at the table, and dined on Spaghetti with meatballs, hot Italian sausage, onions, peppers, mushrooms, and kiwi lemonade.

Chapter 86

"Who is it?" Jordan yelled from the kitchen.

"It's Gladys Jordan," Grandma yelled through the door. I knew I had to get up, so I sat up on the edge of the bed and put on my slippers. Just as I stood, I could hear my grandmother on her way down the hall towards our bedroom.

"I'm up Grandma," I yawned as I started to walk down the hall to meet her halfway and turn her back towards the kitchen.

"I need to talk to you," she said matter-of-factly."

"I know," I said as I sat down at the kitchen table.

"Jordan, can you give us some privacy?" she asked.

"Sure," he said as he turned to leave...

"I'd rather he didn't," I said.

"I'm not going to hurt you Trenice," she said.

"Oh, I know that," I laughed.

"Watch it Trenice," she said.

"Jordan, can you make us some coffee?" I asked.

"Okay," he sighed.

"Okay Grandma, let's talk," I said.

"I'm waiting for Jordan to give us some privacy," she said.

"Fine with me," he said as he rolled his eyes and placed two cups of coffee on the table.

"Thank you," we both said in unison.

"You're welcome," he said as he took his tea, went into the living room, and turned on the television. I was relieved when I heard ESPN.

"You were really disrespectful the other day Trenice," she said matter-of-factly.

"You're right," I said as I started drinking my coffee.

"Don't you think you owe me an apology?" she asked.

"Not really," I said coolly.

"Okay," she said.

"So is that what you came over here for? An apology?" I asked.

"That's one of the reasons," she said.

"Okay," I said.

"Let me explain something to you Trenice," she said as she inched closer to me, drinking her coffee, making me wonder if she was going to hit me upside my head… "That man, good or bad, was the love of my life. When you were born, I was so happy I had a granddaughter, but as soon as I saw you and that damn birthmark, everything changed…" I watched her as tears came to her eyes and she drifted off in thought…

"What changed Grandma?" I asked, as though I didn't know what the answer was…

"I was happy I had a granddaughter, but in that instant, I hated your mother."

"My mother said she didn't know."

"Oh so you talked to your mother?"

"Yea."

"At that moment, it didn't matter what she said or what she knew – All I knew was that she – as you so eloquently put it the other day – fucked my man!" she said angrily.

"You didn't believe her?"

"It didn't matter – she still fucked my man."

"That's not what I asked you."

"At first, I didn't believe her – but then, when she told me how they met, I knew she was telling the truth."

"Why did you tell Miss April and Miss June?"

"Char is your best friend isn't she?"

"Yea."

"Don't you confide in her?"

"Yea."

"Well then you should understand. I know I'm your grandmother Trenice, but I'm also a woman, just like you – I have feelings and I have shit I have to deal with too – every time I see your mother I'm reminded of that shit!" she yelled. I saw Jordan out the corner of my eye peeking into the kitchen listening to our conversation.

"Why did you tell Aunt Trudy?"

"I was hurt and I was angry. Maybe I shouldn't have told Trudy but I did – so what?"

"Grandma you see how Aunt Trudy treats me..."

"Don't you dare blame that on me!" She interrupted.

"I'm not blaming it on you – at least not entirely," I mumbled.

"What the fuck did you say?"

"Well, Grandma, maybe..."

"Maybe what?" she interrupted.

"Maybe if you didn't tell her, she might not be so damn mean!" I laughed.

"You need to see her point of view Trenice."

"Grandma, I love you dearly, but I don't have to see a damn thing when it comes to Aunt Trudy – I'm so fucked up behind all this shit I can't even see my damn self!" I yelled.

"What the hell are you talkin' about Trenice?"

"You knew, Miss April knew, Miss June knew, my mother knew, and Aunt Trudy knew – you all knew about the black sheep – the ugly secret – the incest!"

"How do you think Trudy feels?"

"I don't give a damn how she feels!"

"That's your fuckin' problem Trenice – you can't see how anybody feels but you! Trudy has to deal with the same shit you're dealing with – every time she sees her sister and her other sister..."

"She is not my sister!" I screamed.

"Look Trenice, whether you like it or not..."

"Why did you come over here Grandma?" I interrupted.

"You want me to leave?"

"No – I don't want you to leave – but why did you really come over here?"

"I know you're hurt and I know you're angry – but you need to know you're not the only one that's hurt and angry – you have a right be be angry, but so do I, and so does Trudy – you wouldn't need anybody to explain this to you if it were Jordan."

"It would never be Jordan, Grandma."

"I didn't think it would ever be Thomas either Trenice." We sat there quiet for a few minutes. I had finished my coffee so I started playing with my cup.

"Grandma?"

"Yea?"

"I'm sorry I cursed at you."

"And I'm sorry I knocked the shit outta you," she laughed.

"No you're not."

"I am Trenice. I shouldn't have done that - but when you said what you said – it just brought me right back to when I first laid eyes on you..."

"Grandma?"

"Yea?"

"You hated me didn't you?"

"Trenice?"

"Yea?"

"I could never hate you. Don't you ever say that shit to me again – do you understand me?"

"Yes Grandma."

"Hi Trenice, Hi Miss Gladys," Char said as she sat down at the table.

"I didn't hear you come in," I said.

"Well, I guess I'll go now," Grandma said as she got up from the table.

"Okay – bye!" I said as I jumped up to give her a hug.

"Damn, you rushing me?" she laughed.

"No, not at all," I lied.

"Good bye Trenice," she laughed as she left.

"Thank God," Jordan said as he came into the kitchen.

"What's wrong?" Char asked.

"Nothing – but it got a little heated," Jordan said.

"I knew that soon as I walked in, Char said. "So what happened?"

"Well, to make a long story short..." I started to say...

"Why you gotta make a long story short?" Char laughed.

"Well, at first I didn't know why she was here, then she started talkin' about that was my fuckin' problem because I couldn't see how anybody else was feeling – I could only see how I was feeling."

"What the fuck is wrong with your grandmother?" Char asked.

"That's what I was thinking too, but now I understand what she's talkin' about."

"You do?" Jordan and Char said in unison.

"Yea. Especially when she said no one would have to explain this to me if it was Jordan."

"It would never be me!" Jordan yelled.

"That's what I said honey – and she never thought it would be Thomas either."

"Oh I get it," Char said.

"Well explain it to me then," Jordan said.

"Well, it's kinda like what Char is going through," I said.

"How so?" Jordan said.

"My grandmother loved Thomas, he got her pregnant, then he fucked her daughter and got her daughter pregnant too."

"I guess so," Jordan said.

"Yea, that is fucked up," Char said.

"She tried to tell me I need to understand how Aunt Trudy feels but I wasn't tryin' to hear that," I laughed.

"I know that's right!" Char said.

"She asked me if I felt I owed her an apology and I told her no," I laughed.

"Then damn! I know she didn't like that," Char laughed.

"I'm surprised she didn't get up and leave when Trenice told her that," Jordan laughed.

"Jordan you were here?" Char asked.

"Yea – Gladys wanted some privacy but she didn't get any," he laughed.

"I did apologize for cursing at her, and she apologized for knocking the shit outta me," I laughed.

"She apologized to you?" Char asked.

"Yea, she apologized and when she said she was sorry Trenice told her, no you're not," Jordan laughed.

"I don't believe her either," Char laughed.

"She said she was really sorry and she shouldn't have done that," I said.

"Then damn! She really apologized!"Char said. "Well at least she didn't try to come up in here tellin' you what you had no business doin'," Char said.

"I asked her if she hated me." I said.

"What did she say?" Char asked.

"She said don't ever ask her that shit again," I laughed.

"I'm glad this shit is over," Jordan said.

"Me too," Char said.

Chapter 87

"We interrupt our regularly scheduled programming to bring you this latest bulletin from News 12. Last week, Dr. Aiden was arrested and charged with attempted rape. According to the Yonkers Police, charges were brought against Dr. Aiden after a patient in the E.R. gave a statement, which was later corroborated by security footage provided by St. Joseph's Hospital. In exchange for a lighter sentence, Dr. Aiden has pleaded guilty and has been cooperating with authorities. Dr. Aiden has been released on bail and has returned to his residence at Hillcroft Towers with his wife and children. He will return to court sometime next month for sentencing. We now continue with our regularly scheduled programming..."

Chapter 88

"This can't be happening..." I whispered as I watched News 12. "How can I be living in the same building as that monster? My dream home just turned into a nightmare," I said as tears streamed down my face. "Jordan will be right back," I told myself as I got up from the sofa and went towards the front door...

"Hey Beautiful," Jordan said as he came inside. He knew something was wrong immediately. Once he saw my face, he pulled me close to him and just stood there, holding me, stroking my hair as I sobbed on his chest. As I continued sobbing, he picked me up, carried me into the living room, and sat down on the sofa while cradling me on his lap. When he reached for the remote I wanted to snatch it from him but News 12 was already telling him everything he needed to know:

"We interrupt our regularly scheduled programming to bring you this latest bulletin from News 12. Last week, Dr. Aiden was arrested and charged with attempted rape. According to the Yonkers Police, charges were brought against Dr. Aiden after a patient in the E.R. gave a statement, which was later corroborated by security footage provided by St. Joseph's Hospital. In exchange for a lighter sentence, Dr. Aiden has pleaded guilty and has been cooperating with authorities. Dr. Aiden has been released on bail and has returned to his residence at Hillcroft Towers with his wife and children. He will return to court sometime next month for sentencing. We now continue with our regularly scheduled programming..."

Jordan watched News 12 intently as they showed video footage of Dr. Aiden exiting the lobby with his wife and children. Dr. Aiden had his head down, his wife was by his side holding his arm, and Jordan caught a brief glimpse of Carl holding the door open for them... "I'll be back in a bit," he said as he got up.

"Jordan, please don't leave me," I whispered.

"I'll be back." he said again as he grabbed his cell phone, his jacket, and his keys.

"Where are you going?" I asked, not really sure I wanted the truth. Jordan left without answering me. When he got to the lobby he went right up to Carl:

"Hey Jordan," Carl said when he saw him.

"Hey Carl... le'me ask you something..."

"Okay."

"Does Dr. Aiden live in this building?"

"Yea, Why?"

"I saw News 12 and I recognized him from the hospital," Jordan answered.

"Yea, he's been here for years."

"How long has he lived here?"

"He and his wife moved in about 10 years ago – they have the penthouse suite up on the 30th floor.

"I'm surprised we never ran into him," Jordan said.

"You won't."

"Why's that?"

"He normally leaves around 4pm before y'all get home and he doesn't come back in here 'till after 2 a.m."

"Hmmm... interesting..." Jordan said, deep in thought. "I never knew he was married or had a family either."

"You one of his patients?"

"Naa..."

"You seem mighty interested in a doctor you barely know," Carl laughed.

"Carl – you have to admit – it's not every day you find out a doctor as well-known as he is and is actually living in your building – and he's been arrested – this is some straight Law & Order shit!" Jordan said.

"Yea, I guess it is," Carl laughed.

"I wonder if his wife will move out."

"Naa... she ain't givin' up her lifestyle."

"She might have to now that he's out of a job."

"Naa... she has more money than he does."

"She's a doctor too?"

"Naa... she's an attorney."

"Hmmm... interesting...," Jordan said again while deep in thought.

"You sure you don't know Dr. Aiden?"

"Not as well as you do!" Jordan laughed. "Hey Ma," he said as my mother came into the lobby.

"This is your mother?" Carl asked.

"This is my mother-in-law, Claire," Jordan answered.

"Ooohhh.... You're Trenice's mother – Hi Ma!" he yelled as he grabbed my mother into a hug.

"Well hi – damn – who the hell are you?" my mother laughed.

"I'm sorry," he laughed as he put her down.

"Nice meeting you sorry," she laughed.

"I'm Carl – nice meeting you too," he laughed.

"Are you always so friendly with visitors?" she asked.

"Sorry about that," he answered. "Jordan and Trenice are so special, they're like family," he said.

"Aww... that's sweet – Jordan is Trenice upstairs?"

"Yea," Jordan answered on his way out the door.

"I guess he was in a hurry," Carl laughed.

"I guess so," my mother said on her way to the elevator.

Chapter 89

"Is that you honey?" I asked as I opened the door. "Oh, hey Ma," I said as she walked in. My mother could tell I was disappointed.

"You don't seem happy to see me," she said.

"I thought you were Jordan."

"You okay Trenice?"

"Yea... I guess...," I lied.

"I saw Jordan downstairs talking to Carl when I came in."

"You did?" I perked up a little.

"Yea – Carl is something else!" she laughed.

"What happened?"

"Jordan said hi Ma so Carl thought I was his mother, then Jordan told him I was your mother – so he says oh you're Trenice's mother – hi Ma – and grabs me into a hug!" she laughed.

"That's Carl," I laughed.

"I said well damn – who the hell are you – he said I'm sorry – I said nice to meet you sorry!" she laughed.

"Oh shit!" I laughed.

"After he told me his name I asked him if he was always so friendly with the guests – he apologized again and said you and Jordan were so special to him y'all were like family."

"That's Carl," I sighed.

"Is he married?"

"Nope."

"Hmmm... interesting...," my mother said deep in thought.

"So what's up?" I asked interrupting her thoughts.

"A lot of shit went down the other day," she answered.

"Yes it did."

"You okay?"

"Okay as I can be I guess..."

"Ma call you yet?"

"She was here yesterday."

"She was?"

"Yea – she said she needed to talk to me."

"Oh boy..."

"She was kinda heated."

"Why? Because you were disrespectful?"

"I wasn't disrespectful."

"Yes you were Trenice."

"No I wasn't – so stop saying that I was."

"I didn't come here to argue with you Trenice."

"Good – 'cause I'm not in the mood."

"Look Trenice..."

"Ma, don't start...," I interrupted.

"I'm not here to – never mind – what did Ma say?"

"Well, first she asked me if I thought I owed her an apology and I said no."

"Trenice!"

"What Ma?"

"What else did she say?"

"I really don't want to tell you."

"Why?"

"Cause I don't want to hurt your feelings."

"What did she say?"

"You sure you want me to tell you?"

"Yea Trenice – tell me."

"Okay. She said Thomas was her man and as soon as she laid eyes on me she knew what happened.

"Okay – what else?"

"She said I needed to see things from her point of view and my fuckin' problem was I couldn't think of anyone but myself."

"Bitch got some nerve comin' over here dumpin' that shit on you – you're not supposed to see things from her point of view – you didn't fuck him – I did!" she yelled.

"See, that's why I didn't want to tell you."

"I'ma give her a piece of my mind when I see her too..."

"Please don't Ma," I interrupted.

"Oh yes the hell I am – I don't give a damn what you say!"

"She said nobody would have to explain things to me if it were Jordan."

"It wouldn't be Jordan!" she yelled.

"That's what I said too – then she said she never thought it would be Thomas either."

"You know what? Now I'm fuckin' pissed – she should have had this conversation with me – not you!"

"I know."

"And she had the nerve to expect an apology from you – fuck her!" she yelled.

"I did apologize to her."

"For what? Like I said..."

"I apologized for cursing at her, and she apologized for hitting me."

"She apologized? To you?"

"Yea. She said she shouldn't have hit me but when I so eloquently reminded her you fucked her man..."

"Wait a minute..." she interrupted as she bust out laughing.

"She said as I so eloquently put it when I said you fucked her man, it just brought her back there so she hit me."

"I'm sorry Trenice," she laughed, "I'm not laughing at you – I'm laughing at how you so eloquently put it..."

"It's kinda fucked up though Ma."

"You don't need to tell me that Trenice – I'm living it."

"Well now I'm living it too, and so is Aunt Trudy."

"Oooohhh... now I get it! Ma didn't give a fuck about you Trenice!"

"Ma don't say that."

"You're right – I shouldn't say that – but she came over here because of Trudy!"

"Yea, I figured that out," I laughed.

"You did?"

"Yea - she got mad when I told her I wasn't tryin' to hear it," I laughed.

"You ARE my child," she laughed.

"Hey Ma, hey Beautiful,"
Jordan said as he came in the door.

"Hey Honey – where'd you go?" I asked.

"Out," he answered as we went into the kitchen.

"I gotta get Bunny from school – I'll see you later Trenice," my mother said as she gave me a hug.

"Aiight Ma, see you later," I said as I hugged her back.

"Bye Jordan," she said on her way out.

"Honey?"

"Yes Beautiful?"

"You need to put this jacket in the cleaners — I don't know where you went but it looks like you got blood on your jacket."

"Gimme the damn jacket," he said as he snatched the jacket from me, snatched his keys, and slammed the door on his way out.

Chapter 90

I could hear the conversation coming from the elevator. My heart sank as I continued to listen:

"I still can't believe it," Aunt Trudy said.

"Me neither," Sissy said.

"What the hell are they doing here?" I asked out loud as I cracked my door.

"Hey Beautiful," Jordan said as he came inside.

"Sssshhhh!" I said as I pulled him inside quickly.

"Who are you listening to?" he whispered as he crept up behind me.

"What floor are we on?" Aunt Trudy asked.

"We're on the 13th floor," Sissy said.

"We were supposed to get off on the 30th floor," Aunt Trudy said.

"Thank God," I whispered.

"Are you sure she's home?" Sissy asked.

"She's always home," Aunt Trudy answered.

"Well I hope she's alright," Sissy said.

"Me too," Aunt Trudy said.

"I don't think I could be in the house with my husband after that shit," Sissy said.

"Jane will stand by Dr. Aiden no matter what he does," Aunt Trudy said.

"She's a better woman than I am," Sissy said.

"I know – he's been cheating on her for years – where is this damn elevator?" Aunt Trudy asked while banging on the elevator door.

"He's been cheating on her?" Sissy asked.

"Hell yea he's been cheating on her – they said somebody claimed he tried to rape them but I know that's a bunch of bullshit!" Aunt Trudy said.

"How you know?" Sissy asked.

"Yea bitch – how do you know?" I mumbled.

"I've worked with Dr. Aiden for over 10 years – he ain't attempt to rape nobody – the lil' bitch probably mad 'cause he stopped givin' her that sugar," Aunt Trudy laughed as the elevator finally showed up. Jordan slammed the door shut as I slumped against the wall and slid down to the floor.

"I gotta get outta here," I whispered.

Chapter 91

"Hey Trenice," Tony said as we entered Grandma's building.

"Hey Tony," I said as we went upstairs to Grandma's house. Jordan didn't bother speaking.

"I don't give a damn what you say Ma – you shouldn't have brought that shit to Trenice – you should'a came to me!" I heard my mother yelling.

"You need to stop treating Trenice like a damn baby Claire," Grandma said. Jordan and I stood outside the door without knocking and continued to listen...

"This has nothing to do with Trenice being a baby – you went over there 'cause you were worried about Trudy," my mother said.

"She's my daughter just like you are," Grandma said.

"And Trenice needed to know how you felt about me sleeping with your man 'cause why?"

"Let me tell you something Claire..."

"No Ma – let me tell you something – I'm the one you're mad at – not Trenice!"

"Damn right I'm mad at you!" Grandma yelled.

"I'm mad at my damn self!" my mother yelled.

"Well you sure could'a fooled me!" Grandma yelled.

"You're so blind with rage anybody can fool you!" my mother yelled. "I told you I didn't know!"

"I know you didn't know – that doesn't matter!"

"What'ya mean that doesn't matter?"

"You had his baby Claire!"

"What the hell am I supposed to do Ma? I can't send her back! I swear to God I wish I never met the man!"

"I wish you never met him either! Bad enough I have to deal with all this shit – Trudy has to deal with Trenice being her sister..."

"Aunt Trudy will never, ever be my sister," I said as I opened the door.

"What the hell do you want?" Grandma yelled.

"Coffee," I said as I went into the kitchen and put the kettle on while Jordan sat down at the table with my mother.

"Hey Ma, hey Grandma," he said.

"Hey Jordan – what brings you here?" my mother asked.

"Trenice needed some air," Jordan said as Aunt Trudy and Sissy came inside.

"Ma! Ma! Where you at?" Aunt Trudy yelled.

"I'm back here Trudy," Grandma yelled back.

"C'mon out here Miss Gladys," Sissy yelled.

"I'm comin' dammit!" Grandma yelled on her way down the hall.

"You makin' coffee Trenice?" Aunt Trudy asked.

"Oh I gotta go," I said rushing outta the kitchen. "Ma, can you finish the coffee?" I asked as Jordan got up from the table.

"Yea Trenice – I got it," my mother laughed as I pushed Jordan out the door.

"What the hell is wrong with her?" Sissy asked.

"Y'all see News 12?" I heard Aunt Trudy ask.

"Yea, I saw it," my mother answered.

Chapter 92

"Honey? Honey where are you?" I yawned as I got out of bed.

"I'm in the kitchen Beautiful," he answered. I could smell the coffee and smiled to myself as I went into the living room, sat on the couch, and turned on News 12:

"We interrupt our regularly scheduled programming to bring you this latest bulletin from News 12. Dr. Aiden was found dead this morning in the parking lot at St. Joseph's Hospital. His body was discovered in his car at approximately 6 a.m. News 12 has determined that Dr. Aiden did not return home after his shift yesterday evening. Dr. Aiden had been arrested and charged with attempted rape, plead guilty, and was scheduled to appear back in court to be sentenced next month. Yonkers Police have no further information at this time. We now continue with our regularly scheduled programming..."

"Oh wow," I whispered as Jordan placed a cup of coffee on the table for me. "Did you hear that?" I asked.

"Mmmm hmmm...," he answered. I watched him smile to himself as he sipped his tea.

"Thank God I don't have to worry about running into him anymore," I said as I finished my coffee.

"Never again Beautiful," Jordan said as he pulled me up from the couch and pulled me into a long, deep, passionate kiss.

"I needed that," I whispered in between kisses.

"Me too," he whispered back.

Chapter 93

"Are you sure about this Trenice?" Jordan asked.

"Yes."

"Okay," he sighed.

"Good morning, Tyler Marshall & Associates, how may I help you?" the receptionist asked.

"I need to make an appointment to see Tyler as soon as possible," I answered.

"May I have your name?"

"This is Trenice."

"Trenice who?"

"May I speak to Tyler please?"

"Just one moment..."

"Hello Trenice," Tyler said as he picked up the phone. "How are you?"

"I need to come see you Tyler," I answered.

"Oh boy..."

"Can I come in today Tyler?" I asked.

"I'm actually on my way to court Trenice – I could be gone all day."

"Never mind."

"This must be serious – you don't sound like yourself – tell you what – we break for lunch at 1 p.m. – can you meet me at the court house on South Broadway?"

"Sure I can – what would you like for lunch?"

"Trenice you don't have to do that."

"Yes she does!" Jordan laughed.

"Well," Tyler laughed, "Since you put it that way, I'll take a cold cut special from Sam's with everything on it."

"Okay Tyler – see you at 1 p.m.," I said. When we got to the court house Tyler was all smiles but once he saw my face his facial expression changed.

"Let's go inside," he said as we followed him to the attorney conference room in the back. While we were eating, Tyler started right in...

"Okay – I can see you're walking so you don't have any broken bones, right?"

"Right," I answered.

"What's going on Trenice?" he asked while putting his hand on my shoulder.

"Have you seen News 12?"

"I watch it every day."

"Did you see what happened to Dr. Aiden?" Tyler looked at Jordan as he continued to eat his sandwich. He continued to watch Jordan until he finished eating his sandwich. Jordan sat there expressionless. Tyler answered my question with a question.

"Did you kill Dr. Aiden Trenice?"

"Are you asking me that as my attorney?"

"I'm asking you that as your friend," he answered as he put his hand on my shoulder again.

"I'm suing St. Joseph's Hospital," I answered.

"What happened? What happened!" Tyler yelled. Jordan gave Tyler a look that let Tyler know he better take it down... "I'm sorry – but I can't stand that son-of-a-bitch!"

"I'm suing St. Joseph's Hospital because they failed to protect me," I answered.

"What? From him? Motherfucker!" Tyler yelled.

"I was the patient," I whispered.

"I'm glad he's dead! I couldn't stand defending that man – oh – sorry – I wasn't supposed to tell you that," he said.

"You defended him?" Jordan asked as he stood up. "How could you defend him?"

"Everything okay in here?" the sergeant asked as he opened the door.

"We're fine," Tyler answered. Once the door was closed, Tyler answered Jordan's question. "About a year ago, Dr. Aiden hired me to defend him. Another woman about your age accused him of rape and he vehemently denied it. I believed him up until she settled out of court."

"What changed your mind about him?" Jordan asked.

"After she came here to pick up her check, Dr. Aiden turned to me and said she got what she wanted – just like the rest of them – and then he smiled – it was pure evil. I knew in that instant he was guilty and now that you're here I know damn well he's guilty – we're going to bankrupt that ass!" Tyler yelled.

"But I'm suing St. Joseph's Hospital," I said.

"I know you are – but you're also going after that motherfucker's estate – fuck 'em all!" he yelled.

"He's dead," Jordan said.

"Doesn't matter – they know what he did and he plead guilty – you filed a police report right?"

"Yes," I answered.

"Good – tell me everything – and don't leave anything out," Tyler said as he started taking notes.

"I was in the hospital for alcohol poisoning," I answered.

"When?"

"About 12 hours before he was arrested."

"Why were you in the hospital for alcohol poisoning?"

"I drank too much."

"Are you an alcoholic?"

"Does it matter?" Jordan interrupted.

"Never mind – sorry – I just asked because when you go to court they're going to try and discredit your testimony."

"I'm not going to court," I said.

"Trenice, don't let this man get away with this!"

"I have to."

"Why?" Tyler asked while putting his hand on my shoulder again.

"Because as soon as you file those papers, my name goes public. My Aunt works for St. Joseph's Hospital, she worked with Dr. Aiden, and she's friends with his wife, who just so happens to live on the 30th floor of my building!" I answered as I threw up my hands.

"Unfuckinbelievable!" Tyler yelled. "That's okay – we can serve the hospital with papers and we can file a claim against the estate – he plead guilty and you filed a police report – the wife will want to settle and so will the hospital – now finish telling me what happened."

"I was unconscious..."

"Wait – you were unconscious?" Tyler interrupted.

"Yes."

"So how do you know what he did to you?"

"I saw him do it."

"I thought you were unconscious?"

"I was."

"Okay – le'me get this straight..."

"I had an out of body experience," I interrupted. I saw everything he did to me and it was all caught on video surveillance."

"Does the police department have the video surveillance?"

"Yes they do."

"How did they know to take a look at the video surveillance?"

"When I was set to leave the hospital, I had to pee so I ran to the bathroom. I wound up in the men's room but I didn't realize it until I heard Dr. Aiden's voice."

"Oh my God Trenice! What happened?"

"I came out the stall with my pants open and when I saw him I started to fix my clothes..."

"You okay?" Tyler asked as he moved closer to me and put his arm around me.

"He called me by my name. He said he remembered me from last night... and then... he... he... smiled..."

"That evil bastard!" Tyler yelled.

"I lost it. I kneed him in the groin and started screaming, security came running, I told them he tried to attack me, the police were called, Jordan damn near got arrested..."

"Wait a damn minute!" Tyler yelled. "Why the hell was Jordan getting arrested?"

"Because he called Trenice a lying bitch and I knocked the shit outta him – that's why," Jordan laughed.

"Why didn't they arrest you?"

"He tried to press charges – there were two officers – one wanted to arrest me, the other one said no one was going anywhere until they got to the bottom of it - besides, they didn't like Dr. Aiden's answer when they questioned him," Jordan answered.

"They questioned him?" Tyler asked.

"They questioned both of us," I answered. "They asked me what I was doing in the men's room and why was my pants down..."

"See? That's that fuckin' bullshit!" Tyler yelled.

"Then Dr. Aiden says yea bitch – why was your pants down – and that's when Jordan hit him," I answered.

"My man – damn right!" Tyler said as they high-fived.

"So then Dr. Aiden tells them he remembered me from last night because he was the doctor on call when I came into the emergency room, then Roy told the police he remembered when Dr. Aiden was in the room with me, my gown was down to my knees – he gave Roy a bullshit story about unwrapping my

IV – so the police asked to see the surveillance tapes," I explained.

"Trenice?"

"Yes Tyler?"

"How did Roy know what was on the surveillance tapes?"

"I told him."

"You told him?"

"Yes."

"You told Roy you were unconscious, you saw what Dr. Aiden did to you – and Roy didn't think you were crazy?"

"Roy remembered what he saw. Once I told him what I saw, he knew he had to get the tapes before they were erased."

"So Roy gave the tapes to the police?"

"Yea." Tyler smiled eerily.

"Trenice?"

"Yes Tyler?" I asked, somewhat perplexed.

"You're going to be a very rich woman," Tyler said as he smiled again... "Oh shoot – it's 1:50 – I need to get back upstairs – thanks' again for lunch – we'll be in touch Trenice," he said as he rushed to gather his papers.

"Thank you Tyler," I said as I shook his hand.

"You're welcome... I wonder who killed him?" he asked on his way out the door. I watched Jordan as he looked out the window and smiled.

Chapter 94

"I'm so sorry you're going through this Jane," Aunt Trudy said as she hugged her.

"I had enough to deal with tryin' to explain to the kids why their father was going to jail – now I gotta deal with burying his ass," she said between sobs.

"How are the kids taking it?" Aunt Trudy asked.

"They're all fucked up behind this shit! First their father was going to jail for attempted rape – now they have to deal with not having a father at all – I had to pull them outta school – they don't even have any friends," Jane cried.

"They don't have any friends?" Aunt Trudy asked.

"The other parents won't let their friends come anywhere near here – they're completely alone – thank God they have each other – and as for me – Trudy, you're the only one that's been here for me."

"What about your parents?"

"They don't give a damn about him – they never wanted me to marry his ass in the first place."

"What about you? What about the kids? Don't they care about their grandkids?"

"The kids are with them now. I could've gone over there too but I have too much to deal with here – I gotta plan his funeral, I gotta settle the estate, I gotta put this place on the market..."

"Jane No! Why are you putting this place on the market?"

"I can't stay here Trudy – I already had to pull the kids outta school – plus, on top of settling the estate – this fuckin' bitch Trenice put in a claim against the estate for over two million – I don't have two million dollars Trudy! What am I going to do?"

"Who?" Aunt Trudy asked.

"Trenice! The bitch he tried to rape that night at the hospital!" Jane cried.

"I'm confused," Aunt Trudy said.

"My husband was on call the night Trenice came into the hospital with alcohol poisoning."

"Oh so he told you about that."

"You knew?"

"I was working that night," Aunt Trudy answered.

"Well when Trenice was being discharged from the hospital, she wound up in the bathroom with my husband."

"Get the fuck outta here!"

"She claimed my husband attacked her in the bathroom."

"What was she doing in the bathroom with your husband anyway?"

"The police asked him the same question."

"Do you think he actually did it?"

"I know he did."

"How do you know?"

"They have video surveillance."

"That's bullshit – they can't put video surveillance in the bathrooms."

"It didn't happen in the bathroom Trudy."

"Where did it happen?"

"It happened in the emergency room the night she was there," Jane whispered. "I saw the video and it made me sick to my stomach – Trenice was unconscious – if Roy didn't come in when he did, my husband was going to rape her," she said as she broke down crying again. "I knew my husband was cheating on me, but I didn't know he was such a monster – now I gotta give this bitch two million dollars – that son-of-a-bitch – if he wasn't already dead I'd fuckin' kill him my damn self!" Jane yelled as she continued to cry on Aunt Trudy's shoulder.

"Where are you gonna go?"

"I'll probably stay with my parents in Peekskill until after I sell this place – thank God I have my own 401k or I'd be broke," Jane said as she continued to cry.

"I gotta go – I'll keep checking on you to make sure you're okay."

"Thanks for everything Trudy – if it weren't for you I don't think I'd make it."

Chapter 95

"Hi Tyler – hold on," I said as Jordan opened the door and we went inside. "I'm gonna put you on speaker," I said as I put the phone on speaker and set it down on the kitchen table.

"I have news Trenice."

"Okay."

"Jane Aiden has agreed to settle your claim for two million dollars."

"Woo hoo!" I yelled as Jordan and I high-fived.

"The hospital isn't willing to settle. You may have to go to court."

"I don't want to go to court."

"I know Trenice – but they don't know that."

"I just want this to be behind us Tyler."

"Have I ever let you down Trenice?"

"No Tyler."

"And I'm not about to start. The hospital knew who they were dealing with after the first complaint – which I told them – they should have fired his ass then – which I also told them – who knows how many other patients he's done this to – and gotten away with it – if they bring this to court Dr. Aiden's employment history will be brought up – and I'll be more than happy to tell them that I represented Dr. Aiden in a previous complaint – which I also told them – that plus the video surveillance will bankrupt that fuckin' hospital! Hello? Hello? Anyone there?"

"Yea Tyler, we're here," Jordan answered.

"Trenice?" Tyler called out.

"Yes I'm here Tyler."

"You still wanna settle for one hundred thousand?"

"Hell no!"

"And that's exactly what I told them! They have 24 hours to get back to me or else!"

"Damn Tyler – you mean business," Jordan said.

"Damn right! Hold on... Yea? Put 'em through... yes this is Tyler Marshall... uh huh... I have my client on the other line... hold on... Trenice?"

"Yes Tyler?"

"One million – do you accept?"

"Yes Tyler."

Okay – hold on... Hello? My client has agreed to settle out of court and accept your offer... I'll have the papers before the end of the day? Very good... Trenice?"

"Yes Tyler?"

"Woo hoo! Didn't I tell you?"

"Yes you did Tyler."

"Can you be here tomorrow morning at 9 a.m.?"

"Yes Tyler."

"Alrighty then – congratulations – see you tomorrow!"

"Wow – you hit the jackpot for three million Beautiful," Jordan said as he came up behind me and kissed me on the back of the neck.

"Two million," I said.

"Oh yea – I forgot – Tyler just hit the jackpot too," Jordan laughed.

"Yes he did."

"What's wrong Beautiful?"

"Nothing," I sighed. "I've been playing lotto faithfully for over 10 years – I always knew I'd hit the jackpot one day – I just never imagined it'd be this way." Jordan pulled me up from the chair, pulled me close to him, and held me as I cried on his chest.

Chapter 96

"Hey Carl," Jordan said as we walked into the lobby.

"Hey Jordan, Hey Trenice," Carl said as Vanessa walked up to us.

"Vanessa!" we said in unison as we all hugged.

"How have you been? Are you enjoying your new home?"

"Very much," Jordan answered as he wrapped his arms around me from behind and kissed me on my neck.

"I guess I got my answer," she laughed as Carl came out from behind the desk.

"You can go right up Vanessa," Carl said.

"Where are you going Vanessa?" I asked.

"I'm going up to the penthouse on the 30th floor," Vanessa answered. "Carl, you have my number right?"

"Yes Vanessa, I have it," Carl answered.

"I'm expecting a lot of people today so make sure you call me as soon as they show up okay?"

"Yes Vanessa," Carl answered.

"What's going on?" I asked.

"The penthouse is on the market – here's a copy of the listing – I gotta hurry upstairs to make sure everything's ready – I don't have much time," she said as she hurried towards the elevator."

"Honey... look... I said as Jordan and I read the listing together..."

"Enjoy a spectacular sunrise and a magnificent sunset from this beautiful 30th floor penthouse with 180 degree views from the east, west, and north, including views of Manhattan and the Long Island Sound. Enjoy spectacular view from every room from floor to ceiling windows. This meticulously maintained three bedroom, three and a half bath enormous 2,570 square foot apartment is move in ready, Large Living Room, separate Dining Area with an Open Floor Plan, Cherry Cabinetry and Granite Counters, SS Appliances, Brazilian Cherry Wood Floors throughout, Juliette Balcony's along with nine foot ceilings. Amenities include 24/7 Concierge, Doorman, Valet Parking, Basketball Court, Indoor Pool, Playroom, Business Center, Owners Lounge, Gym, and Spa. Only 35 minutes to Grand Central Station."

"Let's go see it," I said.

"Are you sure Trenice?"

"Yes."

"You know Dr. Aiden lived there."

"I know."

"And you still want to go see it?"

"Yes..." I sighed.

"Okay... Carl?"

"Yea Jordan?" Carl answered.

"Call Vanessa and tell her we want to come upstairs and see the penthouse," Jordan said.

"You sure about that?"

"Yes Carl," I answered.

"You know how much their asking?" Carl asked.

"Call Vanessa man," Jordan said.

"Hello Vanessa? Yea – Jordan and Trenice wanna come upstairs and see the penthouse... okay... hold on... she said it's by appointment only and..."

"Give me the phone," I demanded as I stood in front of Carl with my hand out...

"Excuse me?" Carl asked. "And just who do you think you're talking to?"

"I'd like to speak to Vanessa... please," I said as I looked at Carl apologetically.

"That's more like it," Carl laughed as he handed me the phone.

"Hi Vanessa – it's Trenice – we'd really like to come see the penthouse," I said.

"I'm sorry Trenice, but the seller has requested serious inquiries only – plus, you also have to have proof of funds – I'm sorry but I really need to finish getting things set up..."

"Please?" I asked.

"Trenice, this is my job..."

"I promise we won't do anything to jeopardize your job Vanessa..."

"Trenice I'm sorry but..."

"Please? We won't stay long – we won't 'cause any trouble..."

"Okay... but make it sound like I stood my ground and let Carl hear you – he can't know anything about this..."

"Okay Vanessa... I understand... thanks' anyway... that's fine," I lied. "C'mon Honey, let's go upstairs," I grabbed Jordan's hand, sighing as if I was disappointed...

"She said no huh?" Jordan asked.

"She said yes – but we need to hurry – c'mon..." I said as we made a beeline for the elevator..."

"Trenice, what's going on?" Jordan asked.

"The seller said serious inquiries only and you have to have proof of funds – she doesn't want Carl to know anything about it so I had to make it sound like she said no..."

"Trenice, have you seen the asking price?"

"Yes," I answered as the elevator doors opened. "Let's go..."

"Hi Vanessa..."Jordan said.

"Listen – you have 45 minutes – you're lucky I like you – I need this listing – don't fuck this up for me – a sista gotta eat," Vanessa laughed. "I'm going downstairs – when I call your phone, get the fuck outta here – got it?"

"Yes Maam!" Jordan laughed as she slammed the door.

"Honey, this is beautiful," I sighed as I went straight for the piano and sat down.

"We don't have time for this Trenice..."

"I know Honey – but I would love to come home to this every evening, play some music on the piano... turn the lights down low, take in the view ..."

"Hmmm... interesting...," Jordan said as he came up behind me, kissing me on the back of my neck...

"You could take me into the dining room, sit me on the table..." I said as he followed me into the dining room and I sat on the dining room table..."

"Hmmm... interesting...," he said as he spread my legs, stood between them, and wrapped them around his back...

"You could chase me from the bathroom, catch me in the guest bedroom ...," I panted as I ran from the guest bathroom, into the guest bedroom, jumped on the bed...

"Hmmm... interesting...," Jordan said as he came up behind ...

"Shit... the phone's rigning... I panted..."

"Jordan? Trenice?" Where are you?" Vanessa yelled as she came toward the master bedroom...

"We're in here," Jordan answered as Vanessa came into the bedroom and eyed us looking out the window, and immediately bust out laughing...

"Y'all are fuckin' crazy!" she laughed. "But you need to get the fuck outta here now."

"Vanessa?"

"Yea Trenice?"

"Do you still have Tyler's number?" I asked.

"Yea Trenice – why?" she laughed.

"Give him a call." I answered.

"Why would I do that Trenice?" she asked.

"Because he can give you proof of funds." I answered.

"Stop playing Trenice," Vanessa laughed.

"She's not playing," Jordan said as he came up behind me and started kissing me on the back of my neck...

"You're serious? Okay – I'll call him later today – woo hoo!" she yelled as we left the penthouse.

"That was close..." Jordan whispered as he pulled me into a kiss in the elevator...

"Yes it was..." I breathed in between kisses...

"To be continued..." he whispered as we got off the elevator and went towards the door...

"My pleasure..." I whispered as we went inside and locked the door.

Chapter 97

"Char! Char! It's Trenice!" I yelled as I banged on the door.

"Why didn't you call first?" she snapped when she opened the door.

"Damn... I'm sorry... I'll come back later," I said as I turned to leave.

"Girl, git in here," she said as she grabbed me into a hug and pulled me back inside. "I need a favor," she said.

"What's wrong Char... you okay?"

"I need to go finish what I was doin' before you banged on the door – help yourself to some coffee!" she yelled as she darted back into the bedroom and slammed the door behind her.

"I ain't mad at you Char – don't stop, git it, git it," I laughed as I went into the kitchen, made myself some coffee, and sat down at the table…

"Shit – I gotta call Jordan," I whispered as I got Jordan on speed dial…"

"Hey Beautiful – where are you?"

"I'm at Char's house," I whispered.

"Oh okay – tell her I said hi…"

"She's kinda busy right now," I whispered.

"Why are you whispering?"

"When I got here she told me she needed to finish what she started," I whispered.

"Who she in there with?"

"I don't know."

"Who the fuck are you talkin' to Trenice?" Char asked.

"Hi Char," Jordan laughed.

"Babe – whose here?" Carl asked as he walked into the kitchen.

"Carl?" Jordan and I said in unison.

"Oh… ahem… Hi Trenice," Carl said.

"Hi Carl," Jordan laughed.

"Hey." Carl said.

"I don't think this shit is funny!" Char snapped.

"The hell it ain't!" Jordan laughed.

"I'm so embarrassed," Carl said as I bust out laughing.

"For what?" Char asked.

"I didn't mean for anybody to hear us," Carl said.

"Honey, can you come over here," I asked.

"I'll be there in a few minutes," Jordan laughed.

"I'm still mad at chall," Char said.

"And I'm still embarrassed," Carl said. "Babe, I'ma take a shower okay?"

"I'm coming with you," Char said as she followed him down the hall...

"Ummm... why don't you stay out here and keep Trenice company?" he asked.

"She don't need no damn company – she's fine – let's go get in the shower," she ordered.

"Ummm... you sure Babe?" Carl asked.

"Tryin'a tell you," Char answered as she pushed him down the hall towards the bathroom...

"Who is it?" I asked as I went to the door...

"It's me Beautiful," Jordan said as I let him in.

"Where are they," Jordan asked as we sat in the living room.

"They're in the shower," I laughed.

"You think Char's still mad at us?"

"Doesn't sound like they're mad to me," I laughed as I pointed down the hall..."

"Oh it's like that... stop it... okay... I'ma tap dat ass real good... you better run..." Carl said.

"You better catch me," Char laughed.

"You talkin' all that shit – now what?" Carl asked as he caught her and grabbed her...

"Stop... okay... okay...," she laughed.

"Git your ass in there," He laughed as they went into the bedroom and slammed the door...

"I never thought I'd see Carl here," Jordan laughed.

"Me either," I laughed.

"I'm glad Char got a good man," Jordan laughed.

"Me too," I laughed.

"You think they remembered we're still here?" Jordan laughed.

"Yyyyyeeeeessssss!" we heard from down the hall.

"I guess that answered your question," I laughed.

"I'll see you later Babe," Carl said as he kissed Char.

"See you later," Char said.

"Wait!" I yelled.

"For what?" they asked in unison.

"We gotta tell you what happened," I laughed.

"Trenice – I need to get to work," Carl said.

"Remember when we wanted to see the penthouse?" I asked.

"Trenice I gotta go," Carl said.

"Give her a minute," Jordan laughed.

"What penthouse?" Char asked.

"On the 30th floor," I answered.

"Yea – Vanessa said you couldn't see it," Carl said.

"Well... we got to see it..." I said.

"Congratulations – I gotta go!" Carl said.

"Give her a minute Carl," Jordan laughed.

"Le'me sit down," Carl said.

"Me too," Char said as she sat down next to Jordan.

"Vanessa said we had 45 minutes and when the phone rang, we had to get the fuck out," I laughed.

"Go 'head to work Carl," Char said.

"I got a few minutes – what happened?" Carl laughed.

"Well... we started in the living room," Jordan laughed.

"Then the dining room," I laughed.

"Then the kitchen," Jordan laughed.

"Then the 1st bedroom," I laughed.

"Then the 2nd bedroom," Jordan laughed.

"Then she shower," I laughed.

"The shower?" Char and Carl asked in unison. That did it...

"AAAAHHHHHHHH...

HA, HA, HA, HA, HA, HA, HA, HA, HA, HA, HA, HA, HA, HA, HA, HA, HA, HA, HA, HA... AAAAHHHHHHHH...

HA, HA, HA, HA, HA, HA, HA, HA, HA, HA, HA, HA, HA, HA, HA, HA, HA, HA, HA, HA... AAAAHHHHHHHH...

HA, HA, HA, HA, HA, HA, HA, HA, HA, HA, HA,
HA, HA, HA, HA, HA, HA, HA, HA, HA...
AAAAHHHHHHHH...
HA, HA, HA, HA, HA, HA, HA, HA, HA, HA, HA,
HA, HA, HA, HA, HA, HA, HA, HA, HA...
AAAAHHHHHHHH...
HA, HA, HA, HA, HA, HA, HA, HA, HA, HA, HA,
HA, HA, HA, HA, HA, HA, HA, HA, HA..."

"Then the Master Bedroom," Jordan laughed.

"Then the phone rang!" I laughed.

"Oh shit!" Carl laughed.

"Did you answer it?" Char asked.

"I didn't hear it," Jordan laughed.

"Neither did I," I laughed.

"And Vanessa came in!" Jordan laughed.

That did it again...

"AAAAHHHHHHHH...
HA, HA, HA, HA, HA, HA, HA, HA, HA, HA, HA,
HA, HA, HA, HA, HA, HA, HA, HA, HA...
AAAAHHHHHHHH...
HA, HA, HA, HA, HA, HA, HA, HA, HA, HA, HA,
HA, HA, HA, HA, HA, HA, HA, HA, HA...
AAAAHHHHHHHH...
HA, HA, HA, HA, HA, HA, HA, HA, HA, HA, HA,
HA, HA, HA, HA, HA, HA, HA, HA, HA...
AAAAHHHHHHHH...
HA, HA, HA, HA, HA, HA, HA, HA, HA, HA, HA,
HA, HA, HA, HA, HA, HA, HA, HA, HA...
AAAAHHHHHHHH...

HA, HA, HA, HA, HA, HA, HA, HA, HA, HA, HA, HA, HA, HA, HA, HA, HA, HA, HA..."

"Wait... I can't...," Carl laughed, doubled over, holding his stomach, with tears in his eyes...

"She caught y'all?" Char laughed.

"No – but she knew what we were up to," I laughed.

"How you know?" Char asked.

"She asked if we got a chance to finish," Jordan laughed. That did it again...

"AAAAHHHHHHHH...
HA, HA, HA, HA, HA, HA, HA, HA, HA, HA, HA, HA, HA, HA, HA, HA, HA, HA, HA...
AAAAHHHHHHHH...
HA, HA, HA, HA, HA, HA, HA, HA, HA, HA, HA, HA, HA, HA, HA, HA, HA, HA, HA...
AAAAHHHHHHHH...
HA, HA, HA, HA, HA, HA, HA, HA, HA, HA, HA, HA, HA, HA, HA, HA, HA, HA, HA...
AAAAHHHHHHHH...
HA, HA, HA, HA, HA, HA, HA, HA, HA, HA, HA, HA, HA, HA, HA, HA, HA, HA, HA...
AAAAHHHHHHHH...
HA, HA, HA, HA, HA, HA, HA, HA, HA, HA, HA, HA, HA, HA, HA, HA, HA, HA, HA..."

"Well – did you finish?" Carl asked while whipping his eyes.

"Yea we did," I laughed.

"Y'all are fuckin' crazy!" Char laughed.

"I never, ever heard of an open house like this," Carl laughed.

"Vanessa told us we were fuckin' crazy too – then she told us to get the fuck out!" Jordan laughed. That did it again...

"AAAAHHHHHHHHH...
HA, HA, HA, HA, HA, HA, HA, HA, HA, HA, HA, HA, HA, HA, HA, HA, HA, HA, HA, HA...
AAAAHHHHHHHHH...
HA, HA, HA, HA, HA, HA, HA, HA, HA, HA, HA, HA, HA, HA, HA, HA, HA, HA, HA, HA...
AAAAHHHHHHHHH...
HA, HA, HA, HA, HA, HA, HA, HA, HA, HA, HA, HA, HA, HA, HA, HA, HA, HA, HA, HA...
AAAAHHHHHHHHH...
HA, HA, HA, HA, HA, HA, HA, HA, HA, HA, HA, HA, HA, HA, HA, HA, HA, HA, HA...
AAAAHHHHHHHHH...
HA, HA, HA, HA, HA, HA, HA, HA, HA, HA, HA, HA, HA, HA, HA, HA, HA, HA, HA..."

"I know she's mad at chall," Char laughed.

"Actually she's very happy," I said.

"She is?" Char and Carl said is unison.

"Yes she is," Jordan laughed.

"I bet y'all made her day," Carl laughed.

"Especially when we told her we were interested," I laughed.

"What?" Char and Carl said in unison.

"We're interested in the penthouse," I said.

"Oh my God! Congratulations!" Carl yelled as he pulled us both into a jug.

"Thanks Carl," Jordan said.

"Yea… thanks Carl… I can't breathe…" I managed to say.

"Oh… sorry Trenice," Carl laughed as he let go of me.

"I'm surprised y'all can afford it," Char said. We all sat there quiet for a few minutes…

"Y'all can really afford it?" Carl asked.

"Yea," I answered.

"How?" Char asked.

"Babe, that ain't our business," Carl said.

"Well?" Char asked again.

"Babe!" Carl said.

"It's okay Carl," I said.

"Well… it's listed for 1.5 million… y'all musta hit the jackpot or somethin'," Carl said.

"I did," I lied.

"What?" Char, Carl, and Jordan said in unison.

"I've been playing lotto for years and I finally hit the jackpot," I lied.

"Hot damn – congratulations!" Carl yelled as he grabbed me into a gentler hug. "So you gonna retire?"

"Not yet," I laughed. "I still gotta work – I only hit for 3 million."

"Well I need to get to work for real now – bye Babe," Carl said as he pulled Char into a kiss.

"Bye," Char said as she kissed him back. "You turn in your ticket yet?" Char asked as Carl left.

"Not yet," I lied. "I'ma wait a couple of days."

"I'm happy for y'all," she said as she hugged me really tight.

"I'm really happy for you too Char," I said.

"How long have you and Carl been dating?" Jordan asked, changing the subject...

"Since y'all left me waiting that day," Char sighed.

"I think you're perfect for each other," I said.

"Me too," Char sighed. "It's been a long time since I've been this happy."

"It's a good look," Jordan said.

"You really think so?" Char asked.

"I know so," Jordan answered.

"Then damn – I know I'm good," she laughed.

"So do we!" Jordan and I said in unison. That did it again...

"AAAAHHHHHHHH...
HA, HA, HA, HA, HA, HA, HA, HA, HA, HA, HA, HA, HA, HA, HA, HA, HA, HA, HA, HA... AAAAHHHHHHHH...
HA, HA, HA, HA, HA, HA, HA, HA, HA, HA, HA, HA, HA, HA, HA, HA, HA, HA, HA, HA... AAAAHHHHHHHH...

HA, HA, HA, HA, HA, HA, HA, HA, HA, HA, HA, HA, HA, HA, HA, HA, HA, HA, HA, HA...
AAAAHHHHHHHH...
HA, HA, HA, HA, HA, HA, HA, HA, HA, HA, HA, HA, HA, HA, HA, HA, HA, HA, HA, HA...
AAAAHHHHHHHH...
HA, HA, HA, HA, HA, HA, HA, HA, HA, HA, HA, HA, HA, HA, HA, HA, HA, HA, HA..."

Chapter 98

"Hello?" I said as I picked up the phone.

"We have a problem Trenice," Vanessa said.

"Hold on – I'm going to put you on speaker," I said as I motioned for Jordan to come listen.

"I lost the listing for the penthouse," she sighed.

"How?" I asked.

"She told the company she felt I wasn't professional and I couldn't be impartial."

"Where is all this coming from?" Jordan asked.

"She found out I showed you the penthouse." Vanessa answered.

"Okay – it was an open house – what's wrong with that?" I asked.

"When I sent over your financials, she was livid – she said she wants nothing to do with me and no way in hell is she selling to you! I knew I shouldn't have let you in... Dammit!"

"Vanessa?" I interrupted.

"Yea Trenice?"

"There's something you need to know..."

"What Trenice? Did something happen between you and Jane?"

"Jane? Who's Jane?" Jordan interrupted.

"Jane is Dr. Aiden's wife," I answered.

"How did you know that Trenice?" Vanessa asked.

"My aunt worked with her husband at St. Joseph's hospital for years – Jane is a good friend of hers," I answered. "Have you been watching News 12?"

"I don't watch it that often," Vanessa said.

"Well... her husband was accused of attempted rape..."

"Oh my God!" Vanessa screamed.

"Then, before he could be sentenced... he was killed..."

"Oh my God!" Vanessa screamed again.

"She has to bury her husband, settle the estate, make sure the kids are okay, sell the penthouse – she hasn't had a chance to catch her breath," I explained.

"I had no idea she was going through so much – I don't know how she's keeping it all together – why is she so adamant that you can't buy her property though? Does she even know you?"

"I'm sure she knows I live in the building – she probably would prefer it were someone else…"

"Did you get any other offers?" Jordan interrupted…

"Actually we got quite a few offers – oh wait – I can't discuss any of that with you…"

"Vanessa?" I interrupted.

"Yes Trenice?"

"We want you to represent us," I said.

"Trenice, I can't do that – I represent the seller."

"That's fine," I said.

"Are you sure Trenice?" Vanessa asked.

"Yes I'm sure," I laughed.

"Okay – I'll need another signed contract from you…"

"That's fine – Tyler can get that over to you later today, if he hasn't already…" I said.

"Trenice, how did you know…"

"I didn't," I interrupted, "But since you sent a blank, Tyler can fill in whatever you need – it's already signed – just let him know," I answered.

"Okay... now, if I can just salvage this listing..." she sighed.

"Vanessa?"

"Yes Trenice?"

"How long was the contract for?"

"30 days – it'll take longer than 30 days to close on her property – people have to get their financing together..."

"Vanessa?" I interrupted.

"Yes Trenice?"

"Tell her I'll give her full asking if she throws in the piano."

"Trenice?"

"Yes Vanessa?"

"You know she wants 1.5 million right?"

"Yes Vanessa."

"Are you sure about this?"

"Yes Vanessa."

"Girl, you are something else," she laughed. "I'ma call you right back."

"Okay Vanessa."

"Are you sure about this Trenice?" Jordan asked.

"Yes Honey."

"That'll take all the money you have," he sighed.

"No it won't" I said.

"How so?" Jordan asked.

"She wants 1.5 million – I have 2 million – we'll have half a million left, plus whatever we get when we sell this place – it's not like we were gonna retire anyway," I said.

"You're right," he laughed.

"Hello?" I answered as I put the phone on speaker.

"Hi Trenice – it's Tyler."

"Hi Tyler," we said in unison.

"I just sent Vanessa all your paperwork – do you want me to make out a certified check out of your settlement?"

"She hasn't accepted my offer yet," I said.

"Why the hell not? Is she crazy?" Tyler yelled.

"She's hurt – and she's bitter Tyler," I answered.

"What the hell does that have to do with you?" he yelled.

"I represent everything she's going through right now Tyler..."

"You're not responsible for the actions of her husband!" Tyler yelled.

"I know – but I am responsible for my own actions," I said.

"What the hell are you talking about Trenice?"

"Well... I filed a claim against her husband's estate..."

"As you should have," Jordan interrupted.

"And now I'm taking her home away from her," I said.

"You ain't taking shit – if it wasn't for her husband…"

"Tyler?" I interrupted.

"Yes Trenice?"

"Logic ain't got shit on the heart," I said.

"Trenice?"

"Yes Tyler?"

"You are something else," he said. "I'll wait 'till I hear from you."

"Okay Tyler," I said as I hung up.

"Hello? I answered again as I put the phone on speaker.

"Hi Trenice – its Vanessa."

"Hi Vanessa," we said in unison.

"I don't believe what just happened," she laughed.

"What happened?" I laughed.

"Well… she really didn't want to sell to you, but you were the only one who offered full asking – and since she wants to get on with her life – she's accepting your offer – and, she's giving you the piano," Vanessa laughed.

"I'm getting the piano too? Yes!" I screamed.

"Trenice – why is the piano so important to you?"

"I've always wanted a piano," I answered.

"Really? You play?"

"We both do," Jordan answered.

"So can you close in two weeks?"

"Sure we can Vanessa," I answered.

"Trenice?"

"Yes Vanessa?"

"I owe you big time!" she yelled.

"You're welcome," I laughed. "Call Tyler and let him know my offer was accepted – he'll take care of everything."

"Okay – see you soon Trenice – love ya!"

"We love you too Vanessa," I said as I hung up.

"She sure is happy," Jordan said.

"She's gonna make between $90 - $120k," I laughed.

"Oh Shit! No wonder she didn't want to lose this deal," Jordan laughed.

"And she's representing us too – so she'll get paid twice," I said.

"Oh shit!" Jordan laughed again.

"And – she's going to represent us on the sale of this place," I laughed.

"No wonder she loves us," Jordan laughed.

"Maybe we should get into real estate," Jordan said.

"Maybe one day we will," I said.

"I'm gonna miss this place," Jordan said.

"I think the penthouse will help us get over it," I sighed.

"I think so too..." Jordan said as he pulled me into a kiss..."

"I can't wait to take a shower..." I said between kisses...

"Hhhhmmmmm.... Interesting..." Jordan said between kisses...

"Hello?" I said as I answered the phone, putting it on speaker.

"You're all set Trenice – I'll make out a certified check to Jane and I'll make out a check to you for the difference - I'll have her come here first so you won't run into each other – I'll see you in two weeks," Tyler said.

"Thank you Tyler."

"You're welcome Trenice."

Chapter 99

"Hi Mom, I said as we walked in.

"Jordan! Trenice!" Shaliyah yelled as she ran up to us, grabbing us into a hug.

"Hi Jordan, Hi Trenice," Mom said as she sat down in the living room.

"What are you guys doing here?" Shaliyah asked.

"We just came over to visit, I answered.

"Trenice, who you tryin' to fool?" Mom laughed.

"Mommy – Trenice isn't trying to fool anybody – she's right here – see?" Shaliyah laughed.

"Yea Mom – see?" I laughed. "Honey – go get Mum Mum."

"Okay Beautiful," Jordan said as he hurried downstairs.

"Trenice, what's going on? Is everything okay?" Mom asked.

"Everything's fine..." I sighed.

"Hey Claire," Miss April said as she came inside and sat down.

"Hey April, Hey June, Mom said.

"Hey," Miss June said as she sat down.

"You okay Mum-Mum?" Jordan asked.

"Yea – just tryin' to catch my breath," she laughed.

"Okay Trenice – everybody's here – what's going on?" Mom laughed.

"We're moving," I said.

"Nooo!" Shaliyah cried. "Where are you going?" she asked while burying her head in my lap.

"We're moving upstairs Shaliyah," I said.

"Why? Did you break another bed?" That did it...

"AAAAHHHHHHHH...

HA, HA, HA, HA, HA, HA, HA, HA, HA, HA, HA, HA, HA, HA, HA, HA, HA, HA, HA... AAAAHHHHHHHHH...

HA, HA, HA, HA, HA, HA, HA, HA, HA, HA, HA, HA, HA, HA, HA, HA, HA, HA, HA... AAAAHHHHHHHHH...

HA, HA, HA, HA, HA, HA, HA, HA, HA, HA, HA, HA, HA, HA, HA, HA, HA, HA, HA, HA... AAAAHHHHHHHH...
HA, HA, HA, HA, HA, HA, HA, HA, HA, HA, HA, HA, HA, HA, HA, HA, HA, HA, HA... AAAAHHHHHHHH...
HA, HA, HA, HA, HA, HA, HA, HA, HA, HA, HA, HA, HA, HA, HA, HA, HA, HA, HA, HA, HA..."

"Y'all done?" Jordan asked.

"Why does everybody laugh when I say that – it's not even funny!" Shaliyah said.

"Yes it is Shaliyah – but it's only funny in cartoons," I said.

"Oooohhh.... Okay.... But why are you moving upstairs?" Shaliyah asked.

"Because it's beautiful..." I sighed.

"More beautiful than where you live now?" Shaliyah asked.

"Yea..." I sighed.

"Upstairs where?" Mom asked.

"The penthouse," I answered.

"Y'all buying a penthouse?" Miss April asked.

"Yes Mum-Mum," Jordan answered.

"I thought there was only one penthouse in your building?" Mom asked.

"That's right," I answered.

"It's on the market?" Miss June asked.

"Not anymore," Jordan answered.

"Y'all bought it?" Mom asked.

"Yea..." I sighed.

"When?" Miss April asked.

"Today," Jordan answered.

"How much were they asking?" Mom asked.

"1.5 million," I answered

"Where in the hell did you get that kinda money?" Mom asked.

"I hit lotto," I lied.

"Woo hoo! We're rich! We're rich!" Mom, Miss April, and Miss June yelled as they began dancing around the living room. Jordan and I watched them for a few minutes before they realized we weren't dancing with them...

"What's wrong Trenice? This should be the happiest day of your life! You finally hit the jackpot! You don't have to work anymore! You're Freeeeeee!" Mom said as she, Miss April, and Miss June high-fived.

"Not exactly," I said.

"Oh boy... sit down y'all," Mom said.

"I only hit for 3 million – half is gone in taxes – the other half went to pay for the penthouse," I lied.

"Oh well – we still rich!" Mom laughed as she, Miss April, and Miss June high-fived.

"What made you buy the penthouse?" Miss April asked.

"We came home one day and Vanessa was in the lobby..." Jordan said.

"Say no more – I know my child," Mom laughed.

"I'm surprised y'all were interested in the penthouse – the condo you have now is beautiful," Miss June said.

"Once Trenice got a copy of the listing, I knew we were going upstairs," Jordan laughed.

"As soon as I saw that piano..." I sighed.

"Piano?" Mom, Miss April, and Miss June said in unison.

"Trenice sat down and started to play it," Jordan said.

"I know damn well you didn't fall in love with the penthouse over no damn piano," Mom laughed.

"You know your child," I laughed.

"Can I go see your piano?" Shaliyah asked.

"Sure you can," I said.

"Don't tell her that Trenice – you know how she is – you're not the one that has to deal with her cryin' 'cause she didn't get her way," Mom said.

"Shaliyah? You wanna go see the piano now?" Jordan asked.

"Can I Mommy? Pleeeeaaasssseee?" Shaliyah whined.

"When can we see the damn piano?" Mom snapped.

"How 'bout right now?" Jordan teased as he jingled the keys.

"Hot damn – let's go!" Mom yelled.

"Coming Mommy!" Shaliyah yelled as we all hurried out the door.

When we got to the lobby Carl was all smiles.

"Hey Carl," I said when we came in through the doors.

"Hey Trenice... Hi Ma!" he said as he grabbed her into a hug.

"Hi Carl," my mother laughed.

"Hey Carl – this is... Jordan started to say...

"No need for introductions," Carl interrupted. "I can see this beautiful woman is your mother," he said as he kissed Miss June's hand... "Or is it this beautiful woman..." he asked as kissed Miss April's hand.

"I'm Jordan's mother," Miss June said as the blushed.

"And I'm Jordan's grandmother," Miss April laughed.

"Hi Ma, Hi Grandma," Carl said as he hugged them both.

You sure are friendly," Miss April said.

"Yes he is," I laughed.

"Y'all come to see the penthouse?" Carl asked.

"We came to see the piano!" Shaliyah yelled.

"And what's your name sweetie?" Carl asked.

"I'm Shaliyah – and you're Mr. Carl," she laughed.

"Yes I am – lovely meeting you too," Carl said as he kissed her hand and she giggled.

"Carl, you wanna come upstairs with us?" Jordan asked.

"No thanks – I have plans," he said as Char came into the lobby.

"Hi y'all – where y'all goin'?" Char asked.

"We're goin' upstairs to the penthouse – wanna come?" I asked like I didn't just hear what Carl said.

"We have plans – bye! Carl said as he whisked Char out the door.

"They're dating now?" Mom asked as we walked to the elevator.

"Yea," I sighed.

"Good for her," Mom said.

"Sure is – he fine!" Miss June said.

"June hush," Miss April laughed as we got into the elevator.

"What floor are we goin' too?" Mom asked.

"30th," Jordan answered. When we got off the elevator, I let Jordan open the door.

"Wow! Look at the piano!" Shaliyah screamed as she ran right to it...

"How'd you get the piano Trenice?" Mom asked.

"I asked for it," I answered.

"You asked for it? And they said yes? Just like that?" Mom asked.

"Yea – besides, she probably didn't wanna have to worry about moving it anyway," I answered.

"She? Who's She?" Miss April asked.

"Dr. Aiden's wife," I answered.

"Oh shit! You bought Dr. Aiden's penthouse?" Mom asked.

"Yes Ma," I answered.

"Isn't that the Dr. that's all over the news?" Miss June asked.

"Yes Mum-Mum," Jordan answered.

"I can't believe my baby got a penthouse," my mother sighed.

"This sure happened fast," Miss April said.

"How did this happen so fast anyway Trenice?" Mom asked as we all followed her from the dining room to the kitchen.

"Oh my God – this is beautiful!" Miss April said as she touched the counters.

"Well – as soon as we saw it, I told Vanessa we'd give her full asking if she threw in the piano," I answered.

"I wonder why she sold it?" Miss June asked as we all went from the kitchen to the 1st bedroom.

"She probably didn't want to stay here with everything going on with her husband," Miss April said.

"Trenice, is this going to be the office?" Mom asked.

"I think so," I answered. "We love the light that comes in here."

"This 2nd bedroom is nice – it's a little smaller – you should make this one the office and that one the guest room," Miss June said.

"Naaa..." Jordan and I said in unison.

"Oh my God – look at the master bath!" Miss April screamed.

"This bathroom is the size of my living room – and look at the shower!"

"Wow – this is gorgeous!" Mom said. Jordan and I just looked at each other and smiled.

"You tell Ma yet?" Mom asked.

"Not yet," I answered.

"She's gonna be so happy," Mom said.

"Well, we better get goin'," Miss April said.

"Okay Mum-Mum," Jordan said.

"Congratulations Baby," Mom said as she kissed me on the cheek.

"Thanks Mom," I said as we all headed towards the elevator.

"We'll get off here," Jordan said when we got to the 13th floor.

"Okay – bye!" Miss June said as she pulled us into a hug.

"Bye Jordan, Bye Trenice!" Shaliyah said as she pulled us into a hug.

"Bye!" Jordan and I said in unison as we all exchanged hugs and kisses. Once we got inside Jordan didn't waste any time...

"You okay Beautiful?"

"I guess."

"What's wrong?"

"I was okay until Mom asked me if I told my grandmother."

"Don't you want to tell her?"

"It's not her I'm worried about."

"Who is it you're worried about then?"

"Aunt Trudy."

"Why are you worried about Trudy?"

"She's friends with Jane – she's not going to be happy about this..."

"Trenice?"

"Yes Honey?"

"Are you happy about this?"

"Yes."

"Are you sure?"

"Sure as I was in the shower," I answered, smiling mischievously.

"Hmmm... interesting...," Jordan said as he pulled me into a kiss.

Chapter 100

Once we got upstairs to Grandma's house I knew it wasn't going to be easy...

"Ma – it's so beautiful!" I heard Mom say.

"I wonder why she didn't tell me?" Grandma asked.

"I'm sure she was gonna tell you Ma," Mom said.

"Where'd she get the money from?" Grandma asked.

"I'll let her tell you herself – Hi Trenice, Hi Jordan," Mom said as soon as we came in and sat down.

"Hi Mom, Hi Grandma," I said as Grandma sat down next to me at the table.

"Hello ladies," Jordan said as he sat down with us.

"I heard y'all bought a penthouse," Grandma said.

"Yea," I sighed.

"Where'd you get the money?" Grandma asked.

"I hit lotto," I lied.

"Whhhaaaattt? Wooo Hoooo!" Grandma yelled as she grabbed me into a hug.

"What's going on?" Aunt Trudy asked as she came in.

"Trenice hit the lotto and bought a penthouse!" Grandma yelled. I just sat there shaking my head. Jordan just threw up his hands.

"What's wrong Trenice? Was it a secret?" Grandma asked.

"No Grandma," I lied…. "Now let's see… where were we… yea – I hit lotto," I said.

"You hit lotto?" Aunt Trudy asked.

"Let the girl talk Trudy!" Grandma said.

"Yea – I still gotta work though," I laughed. So far, that was the only thing I said that was true.

"Shit – you hit lotto for 10 million and you still have to work?" Grandma asked.

"No Grandma – I only hit for 3 million," I lied.

"I thought the jackpot was 10 million?" Grandma asked.

"I hit a couple a months ago when it was 3 million," I lied.

"Ohhh... so that's where you got the money for the penthouse," Grandma laughed.

"Yea," I lied.

"What penthouse?" Aunt Trudy asked.

"In her building on the 30th floor," Mom answered.

"You bought Dr. Aiden's penthouse?" Aunt Trudy asked.

"Yea." I said.

"How much you pay for it?" Aunt Trudy asked.

"Why you so damn nosy?" Jordan asked.

"You know what – fuck you!" Aunt Trudy yelled.

"Miss Gladys I'm sorry," Jordan said.

"For what?" Grandma asked.

"For disrespecting your house," Jordan said.

"You haven't disrespected my house Jordan," Grandma said.

"I haven't yet – but I'm about to," Jordan said as he stood up.

"Whatchu gonna do muthafucka?" Aunt Trudy asked.

"Trudy! What the hell is wrong with you?" Grandma asked.

"I'll tell you what's wrong with her – she's a miserable bitch and she needs to get a fuckin' life!" Jordan said.

"You know what? You can kiss my ass muthafucka!" Aunt Trudy yelled.

"Don't nobody want it!" Jordan yelled.

"Trudy! Are you crazy?" Mom yelled.

"Trenice is a fuckin' liar!" Aunt Trudy yelled. Jordan and I just sat back down. He looked at me and I looked at him. We both knew what was coming next...

"Trudy! What the hell is wrong with you?" Grandma yelled.

"Y'all put Trenice up on a fuckin' pedestal like she's an angel and she can do no wrong y'all don't know the half of it – but since y'all wanna jump all over my ass I'm gonna tell you!" Aunt Trudy yelled.

"Tell me what Trudy?" Grandma asked as she inched closer to Aunt Trudy. I got up, went in the kitchen, put the kettle on, and started making coffee...

"Trenice ain't hit no got damned lotto!" Aunt Trudy yelled. "She sued Dr. Aiden and got 2 million dollars – Jane had to deal with her husband getting arrested – she had to deal with her husband getting killed – she had to settle their estate – she had to pull the kids out of school – now Trenice is taking her penthouse away from her – Jane doesn't deserve any of this shit!" Aunt Trudy yelled. I made three cups of coffee but at that moment, I couldn't pick them up. I couldn't move. I was barely breathing.

Jordan came into the kitchen and pulled me close to him from behind.

"You okay?" he whispered. I just shook my head no. "I got this," he said as he picked up two cups of coffee and sat one cup in front of Grandma and the other cup in front of Mom. I stayed in the kitchen for a few more minutes. I took two glasses from the cabinet, and set them on the counter. After looking in the refrigerator, I found a 2 liter bottle of Pepsi, went in the freezer, put some ice in the two glasses, and started pouring.

"She okay?" Mom whispered to Jordan. Jordan shook his head no. I came out the kitchen with my coffee and set it on the table first, and then I went back into the kitchen and came out with the two glasses of Pepsi. I set one on the table in front of Jordan, and then I threw the other one in Trudy's face. Before she stood up to slap me, I went in:

"Fuck your friend! Maybe she doesn't deserve any of this shit – but I didn't deserve what happened to me either!" I screamed.

"Alright – that's enough!" Grandma yelled as she got in between us and pushed me away from Aunt Trudy. "Y'all can both get the fuck outta my house!"

"I could – but I won't," I said as I sat down and started drinkin' my coffee.

"You lucky Ma's here or I'd bust your ass!" Trudy yelled.

"Oh no you wouldn't either!" Mom and Jordan said in unison.

"What the fuck is Trudy talkin' about Trenice?" Grandma yelled. "Did you hit the lotto or not? And who the fuck is Jane?"

"Jane is Dr. Aiden's wife," Mom answered.

"Dr. Aiden? The one that was on News 12?" Grandma asked.

"Yea Ma," Mom answered.

"He's dead," Grandma said. What's he got to do with this?" Grandma looked Aunt Trudy directly in the eye, but Aunt Trudy wouldn't answer Grandma's question.

"Ma – before Dr. Aiden was killed, he was arrested for attempting to rape one of his patients – which he plead guilty to!" Mom explained.

"Oh my God... not Trenice...," Grandma whispered.

"Yea Ma," Aunt Trudy said sarcastically. "That's where she got her money and that's how she got Jane's condo – I told you she's a fuckin' liar," she laughed.

"Is that true Trenice?" Mom asked as she put her arm around me and pulled me into a hug. She looked in my eyes and already knew the answer.

"Bam!" Jordan, Mom, and I were all in shock when we turned around and saw Aunt Trudy on the floor.

"Ma...," Aunt Trudy tried to speak...

"You knew what that bastard did to your niece and all you care about is your fuckin' friend? Get the fuck outta my house Trudy!" Grandma yelled. Aunt Trudy got up off the floor, left Grandma's house, and slammed the door so hard the dishes shook in the china cabinet. Jordan jumped up and ran out right behind her. Aunt Trudy was pale as a ghost when Jordan caught up to her at the bottom of the stairs…

"Do I have your attention Bitch?" Jordan asked. He had his hands wrapped around her throat too tight for her to speak. All she could do was nod her head. "Very good – now that I have your attention – let me make myself perfectly clear – you live on the strength of your mother – Miss Gladys - I don't give a fuck about you one way or the other – I could snap your fuckin' neck right now - watch you drop to the ground - and step over your ass the same way I do to keep from stepping in dog shit! You have two choices – you can continue to live, or you can disappear permanently – I'ma let go of your throat now – choose wisely," he growled.

When he let go of her throat, she bust out laughing. Jordan stood there as she continued to laugh hysterically. "Muthafucka you think you gangsta?" she asked as she continued to laugh. "You don't scare me!"

"I didn't scare Dr. Aiden either," Jordan said calmly.

"What's that supposed to mean?" she asked as her laughter quickly turned to fear.

She froze as Jordan stepped closer to her, turned her towards the cold cement, turned her face to the left, pushed her face and body up against the cold cement, and held her body against the cold cement with his body as he held her arm held behind her back, and whispered in her ear, "It means I don't need you to be afraid of me to make you disappear." Jordan laughed mischievously to himself as Aunt Trudy snatched the door and ran out the building. When Jordan got back upstairs and opened the door, Grandma was so angry she was shaking...

"I'm sorry Grandma," I said.

"For what?" Grandma asked.

"I dunno," I answered.

"You have nothing to be sorry for," Grandma said. "I'm so mad at Trudy I could fuckin' kill her!"

"Calm down Grandma," I said.

"Don't tell me to calm the fuck down Trenice!" Grandma yelled.

"Turn up Grandma," I said as I got up and started dancing to imaginary music and we all bust out laughing.

"Are you okay Trenice?" Mom asked.

"Yea," I answered.

"Le'me ask you something Trenice," Grandma said. "When did this happen?"

"When I was in the hospital for alcohol poisoning," I answered.

"Oh my God!" Mom screamed.

"Did they catch him?" Grandma asked.

"I don't want to talk about that anymore," I answered.

"I'm glad the bastard's dead – I don't give a fuck about Trudy's friend – I wish I knew who killed him so I could thank him!" Grandma yelled. I looked up at Jordan and saw him smiling mischievously to himself.

"Me too Ma!" Mom yelled.

"So you bought the penthouse with the money you got from suing him?" Grandma asked.

"Yes Grandma," I answered. We sat there quiet for a few minutes and then Grandma started laughing uncontrollably. When she started coughing, I started patting her on her back. Jordan and my Mom just sat there watching us.

"What's so funny Grandma?" I asked.

"You are something else," she laughed. "You're the only bitch I know that can bankrupt a dead man!" she hollered.

"Trenice?" Mom asked. "What made you buy the penthouse?"

"It's beautiful..." I sighed.

"It doesn't bother you?" Mom asked.

"Ma, when we went to see it, we fell in love all over again," I sighed.

"We sure did," Jordan said as he pulled me into a kiss.

"Damn – this must be some penthouse," Grandma said.

"It is..." I sighed.

"Claire?" Grandma asked.

"Yea?" Mom answered.

"How did you know so much about Dr. Aiden?" Grandma asked.

"I worked with him at the hospital before Trudy got there," Mom answered. "Trudy and Jane have been friends for years."

"I wonder if Trudy's ever been to Jane's penthouse," Grandma asked.

"She was there with Sissy a few weeks ago," I said.

"What?" Mom and Grandma said in unison.

"With Sissy? Grandma asked.

"Yea – we heard them talkin' in the hallway while they were waitin' for the elevator," Jordan said. "They were checking on Jane to make sure she was okay."

"You mean to tell me – Trudy came to your building – knowing damn well what happened to you – she gets in the fuckin' elevator – goes upstairs to the penthouse to make sure her fuckin' friend is okay – but she never bothered to check on you? Where did I go wrong with her?" Grandma asked as she put her head in her hands...

"Ma, don't stress yourself – Trudy's gonna be Trudy," Mom said.

"Thank God you're okay Trenice," Grandma said as she pulled me into a hug.

"Me too Grandma," I said.

"I'm surprised Trudy didn't put you on blast sooner," Grandma laughed.

"Oh please – Trudy only kept her mouth shut 'cause she didn't want to tell Jane's business," Mom laughed.

"It was gonna come out sooner or later," I said.

"I see why you didn't tell Ma," Mom laughed.

"I don't," Grandma said.

"You don't understand Ma?" Mom asked.

"Of course I understand Claire – but Trenice didn't have to lie to you, me, or anybody else," Grandma said.

"I didn't have to tell you the truth either," I said.

"What the hell was she supposed to do Ma?" Mom asked.

"I don't know Claire," Grandma sighed.

"Exactly!" Mom said.

"So when are you moving in?" Grandma asked.

"We're gonna move in next weekend," Jordan answered.

"So when can I see this penthouse?" Grandma asked.

"How 'bout right now?" Jordan teased as he jingled the keys.

Carl and Char were all smiles when we got to the lobby. "Hi Guys!" Carl said when he saw us. "Hi Ma! And who is this lovely lady?" Carl asked as he kissed Grandma's hand.

"I'm whoever you'd like to me to be," Grandma laughed.

"Where y'all goin?" Char asked.

"We're takin' Grandma to see the penthouse," I answered.

"Grandma?" I thought you and Ma were sisters!" Carl exclaimed.

"Thank you Carl," Grandma laughed. Are you always this friendly?"

"Yes he is!" Jordan and I said in unison.

"Why don't y'all come upstairs with us this time?" Jordan asked.

"Okay – c'mon Babe," Carl said as he took Char by the hand and we all headed towards the elevator.

When we got upstairs, Grandma was in shock. "Oh my God! It's so beautiful!" she yelled.

"Told you," Mom said.

"It is beautiful," Char said.

"I didn't realize it was this big," Carl said. "I still can't believe you hit lotto and got enough money to buy this place."

"Yea – me either," Grandma said with a smirk.

"They let you keep the piano?" Carl asked.

"Yea…," I sighed.

"I'm so happy for y'all," Carl said. "I was worried for a minute."

"Why Carl?" Mom asked.

"I was worried some snob was gonna come in here and act as if I was his personal doorman," Carl laughed.

"Y'all deserve it," Grandma said.

"Thanks Grandma," I said.

"Well – we better get going – I need to get back to the lobby – you comin' babe?" Carl asked Char.

"Not yet," Char laughed.

"Awww shit!" Mom and Grandma said in unison.

"Now I see where Trenice gets it from," Carl laughed.

"Let's get home before it gets dark Ma," Mom said.

"Okay Claire – bye y'all," Grandma said as she grabbed us into a hug.

"Bye," we said as we hugged her back.

"My turn," Mom said as she grabbed us into a hug.

"My turn," Char said as she came towards us but Carl beat her to it…

"My turn!" Carl laughed as he grabbed us into a hug.

"Is it my turn now? Char laughed.

"Yes Char," we laughed as we all hugged. Once everyone left, Jordan and I just stood in the living room looking out the window.

"I'm glad that's over," Jordan sighed as he pulled me close to him.

"Me too," I said. "Me too."

"Surprise!" everyone yelled as I came in the door.

"Welcome to your shower!" Char yelled as she 'misted' me with water from a squirt bottle as everyone laughed.

"That feels kinda good – gives me an idea," I laughed as I sat down.

"Is that all you ever think about Trenice?" Rachel laughed.

"You have to ask?" Char asked as everyone else laughed.

"Well... since you asked... in a word..."

"Hell yea!" everyone yelled. We all bust out laughing as I got up to go towards the stereo.

"Where you goin'?" Char asked.

"To get this party started," I said as I went over to her stereo, turned it on, set it for CD, and bent down to turn on the subwoofer.

"Trenice, the CD player is up there," Rachel said.

"I know – I'll get to that in a minute – I gotta make sure we don't blow her speakers," I said as I turned on the stereo below and pushed in the button for the subwoofer.

"Blow her speakers? The only way I know to keep from blowin' speakers is to keep the music down," Tish laughed.

"Well," I said as I closed the door, picked up the remote for the CD player, and turned on the music, "with a subwoofer you don't have to worry about that."

"You don't?" Theresa asked.

"No – the subwoofer takes the bulk of the bass and relieves the pressure off the speakers," Sherrie said.

"Thank God – I hate when I go in the club and they have those big-ass speakers in the corner of the room – you ever stand next to one of those?" Monique asked.

"Hell yea – you deaf for about an hour after you leave the club!" Roberta yelled.

"I know – especially on Raggae Night," Diana laughed.

"Well I have a big stereo and big speakers so I don't have to worry about that – my neighbors curse me out every Sunday morning," Carolyn laughed.

"Why Carolyn?" I asked.

"Cause I start playin' my shit nice 'n loud at 7 a.m.," she laughed.

"Damn Carolyn – that's fucked up – why you do that?" Char asked.

"'Shit - they don't mind wakin' me up at 7 a.m. on Saturday morning with their music so I don't mind wakin' them up at 7 a.m. on Sunday with mine," she laughed.

"Shit – I don't blame you Carolyn – I think I should start doin' that shit too – my neighbors always wake me up on Saturday mornin' cussin' at their kids," Tish said.

"Shit – I probably wake up everyone in the building cussin' at my kids," Sherrie laughed. "They whine and cry all week talkin' 'bout they tired and don't want to get up for school, then on Saturday mornin' instead of sleepin' like they have some damn sense or watching TV until I get up, they wanna start fightin' so I gotta get up and start cussin' and beatin' they ass!" she yelled as we all laughed.

"I know – my mother used to do that to us all the time – I hated that shit – she'd grab the broom or whatever she saw talkin' bout' didn't I tell y'all to knock that shit off!" Theresa said as she started rubbin' her leg.

"Shit you think you have it bad? I gotta get up at the crack of dawn on Saturday 'cause my fuckin' cats wanna jump on my face or in my hair and I gotta throw 'em 'cross the damm room!" Roberta yelled.

"Get the fuck outta here!" Diedre said as we all laughed.

"I'd knock the shit outta them damn cats too," Monique said.

"I do – they come right back on the bed too – I can almost picture them laughin' at me talkin' 'bout they scared the shit outta me or somethin'" Roberta said as we all hollered.

"See that's why I don't have cats – I have a dog," Wanda said.

"Yea – and I don't have either one – 'cause they both work – I ain't gotta walk nothin' and I aint gotta clean no litter box," Monique said.

"Oh girl shut the hell up – you don't have nothin' 'cause yo' ass is mean!" Carolyn yelled as we all hollered.

"Damn Carolyn that's fucked up – but true," Bunny laughed.

"Well I don't have any of those problems – I just have Jackass-Joe talkin' 'bout baby you gonna fix me somethin' to eat or baby you gonna fix me some coffee," Theresa laughed.

"So what do you do when he wakes you up talkin' 'bout make him somethin' to eat or make him some coffee?" Char asked.

"I kick his ass out the bed, tell him leave me the fuck alone and let me get some damn sleep - I aint gotta get up early today it's my day off - then I turn over and go back to sleep!" We all hollered again.

"I bet Trenice gets right up — don't you Trenice?" Rachel asked.

"Yea right — 'magine that," I laughed.

"Trenice you full o' shit an' you know it," Char laughed.

"Char when you call me Saturday morning — first of all — do I answer the phone?" She sat there and thought for a minute...

"Oh you right Trenice — I don't even know why I asked..."

"You never get up and make Jordan something to eat or make him coffee Trenice?" Sherrie asked.

"Of course I do — but that's only if I'm already up — and I'm not otherwise engaged," I laughed.

"Otherwise engaged? Could you be more specific?" Diana asked.

"In other words, if you up early either ya makin' breakfast or ya gettin' busy," Sherrie laughed.

"Exactly!" I yelled as we all hollered.

"Let's eat y'all," Char said as we headed to the kitchen to get our eat and drink on.

"Char? Where da koolaid? Girllll... you know you gotsta have koolaid 'cause everybody don't drink!" I said in a southern drawl voice while everyone else bust out laughing.

"I swear – you sound just like Miss Birdie!" Bunny said as we all laughed, holding our stomachs.

"I can't believe she's still around – I thought she was retiring' and movin' to South Carolina?" Carolyn laughed.

"Girllll... you know I ain't leavin' New York 'till I git back all the money they owe me from them damn numbers – shit I need it to buy da house!" Char said in a southern drawl while we all laughed so hard we were falling on the counter.

"Good thing she don't know where you live or she'd be here talkin' 'bout le'me get some a dat for it's gone," I laughed.

"Was she invited?" Tish asked.

"You don't invite Miss Birdie – hear her tell it – she makes the party – if she ain't there..."

"You ain't have no damn party!" we all hollered.

"Well let's eat – Char ain't got no koolaid so I guess I'll settle for some ginger ale," I laughed as I poured myself some ginger ale and went back into the living room.

"Girl you ain't drinkin'?" Theresa asked.

"Naa... I ain't drinkin'" I said as I sat down.

"Oh hell no – Trenice ain't drinkin' at her own party? Girl you know it's tradition to get drunk at your party – here," Roberta said as she handed me a glass of 151 and coke.

"No thanks – I'm good with the ginger ale," I said as I set the glass down.

"Trenice what's wrong?" Bunny asked.

"Nothin' – why?"

"Why? The one who always takes the drink that we can't take 'cause we drunk before we finish the first one? The undefeated 99 Banana champion? You don't wanna drink? What the hell is goin' on?"

"I just don't wanna drink – nothin's going on," I said as I picked up the glass of ginger ale to take a sip.

"Shit girl – you aint foolin' nobody – whatchu got in this glass," Monique said as she snatched the glass from me and took a sip.

"Damn girl – you ain't put nuthin in here," she said as she went and sat back down. The music was playing but nobody was saying anything. Char and Rachel looked at each other and shook their heads. Damn.

"Oh I know somethin's up now – these two shakin' their heads was a dead giveaway – whats up Trenice?" Wanda asked as she inched closer to me as if I was going to whisper in her ear.

"You really wanna know?" I asked as everyone else got closer. Char and Rachel stood in the corner looking at me as if they couldn't believe what I was about to do. Little did they know... "Well... I'll tell ya..."

"What? What? What!" Tish yelled as they all got closer to me.

"I have plans for later," I whispered as I finished my food and swallowed the last bit of ginger ale.

"And?" Diana asked as they tried to inch in even closer.

"And... I want to have all my wits about me," I said.

"What the hell's that got to do with anything?" Carolyn asked.

"You just don't get it do you?" I asked.

"Frankly, no," Diedre said.

"Well I know you all pretty well."

"And?" Diana asked.

"And, I know you're going to give me some toys to play with," I laughed.

"Damn girl – you afraid of passin' out before you get to try 'em all? Whatchu tryin'a do – have a 24-hour marathon?" Sherrie asked as we all bust out laughing.

"I guess you all know me pretty well too," I laughed, silently thanking God they bought it.

"Took you long enough," Char laughed.

"Well let's have some cake," Rachel said as we all headed back to the kitchen and she took the top off the box. I started to cry immediately.

"You don't like it Trenice?" Char asked as she put her arm around me thinking I needed to be comforted.

"Where did you get those pictures?" I whispered as I pointed to the cake. Rachel stood there smiling as everyone else came up to the box to look at the cake.

"Awwww...." They all said as I wiped my eyes.

"You two looked so cute," Roberta said.

"I can't believe you're both on tricycles," Sherrie said.

"You're gonna have adorable children," Tish said.

"Look at the curls in your hair," Monique said.

"Look at Jordan's little sock and shoes!" Diana said.

"I can't believe the detail on the tricycles," Carolyn said.

"They even picked up the colors in the handle bars and wheels," Wanda said.

"Look at streamers in different colors coming down," Diedre said as she pointed to the icing.

"Oh my God – look at your tiny little fingers wrapped around the string on your balloon!" Bunny said as she pointed to the detail in my hand. You could see each of my tiny little fingers wrapped around the string.

"How old were you in this picture Trenice?" Bunny asked.

"I was 5 years old when that picture was taken," I said with tears in my eyes. "How did you get our pictures Char?"

"Miss Gladys and Miss April gave them to me," Char said.

"I'm surprised they didn't tell you what we were up to," Rachel said.

"I don't wanna eat it now," I said just as Char was about to start cutting it.

"I don't wanna eat it either – it's really cute – but we took a picture so you don't have to worry," Char said as she was about to cut the cake.

"Wait!" I yelled.

"Ok Trenice – but we gonna eat it today right? Cause I ain't got room in my freezer for it," she laughed along with everyone else.

"Yes we will eat it – but I want the men to see it first.

"What?" they all yelled in unison.

"Trenice – you invited Jordan?" Char asked.

"Yes."

"Why Trenice?" Rachel asked.

"You'll see when they get here," I said.

"They? Who's they?" Bunny asked.

"All of them."

"All of them?" Tish asked.

"Yes."

"You had this planned all along didn't you?" Char asked.

"No."

"So when did you plan it?" Rachel asked.

"I planned it at the last minute."

"Well I sure hope we don't regret this," Sherrie said. "I told Harold he had to watch the kids so he'll probably bring 'em here," she laughed.

"No he won't – he's gonna drop them off at your mother's later on," I laughed.

"Damn! You really did have this planned didn't you?" Diana asked.

"Yea," I laughed.

"What are you up to Trenice?" Theresa asked.

"You'll see," I laughed.

"Trenice?"

"Yes Char?"

"Did you invite your mother or your grandmother or Jordan's mother or Jordan's grandmother?"

"Hell No!" I laughed.

"I just figured I'd ask," she laughed.

"Shit – we can't be open with them around!" Wanda laughed.

"I know that's right – I could see Miss Gladys now," Carolyn laughed.

"Shit – after what happened with the nightie Miss Gladys would probably tell Trenice – oh no – save this one for the wedding night," Char hollered.

"What happened with the nightie?" Theresa asked.

"Well I had it in the bag but before I could get out the front door, my grandmother pulled it out the bag," I said.

"Oh my God – what did you do Trenice?"

"I didn't get a chance to do anything – she picked it up, looked at it, and told me my grandfather wouldn't like it 'cause it was too open – he preferred to feel his way around," I hollered.

"Girl, you lyin!" Monique said as everyone bust out laughing.

"No I'm not either," I laughed.

"Damn – Grandma's open like that?" Diana asked.

"Y'all startin'a feel that liquor a little huh?" I laughed.

"Hell yea!" Bunny hollered as we all bust out laughing.

"Ok – it's time to open the gifts," Char said as she brought them into the living room and placed them at my feet.

"Get me a paper plate, scissors, and some tape," Rachel said as Char left to go get them. "We need these to make your hat," Rachel said as Char came back into the living room.

"Char? What's that?"

"What Trenice?"

"That thing in the corner – you know – the thing that looks like a camera on a tripod," I laughed.

"Damn – you weren't supposed to see that," she laughed.

"Well since I've seen it – move it a little closer," I laughed.

"Whose gift you wanna open first?" Rachel asked.

"Doesn't matter," I said as she handed me a shoe box. I tore off the paper and handed it to Rachel so she could take a piece of it for my hat and took the top off the box. As I opened the tissue paper in the box I saw 7 pairs of panties in red, yellow, pink, powder blue, peach, lavender, and white.

"Oh – those are nice!" Wanda said.

"To Trenice – wear 'em well girl! Love, Diedre," I read as everyone else laughed.

"Next" Rachel said as she waited for me to tear the paper off my next gift so she could get a piece of the paper and the bow.

"Oh these are nice!" I yelled as I tilted the box so everyone could see I got 7 pairs of sexy sandals to match the 7 pairs of panties Diedre gave me.

"From one sexy woman to another! Love, Char," I read.

"Where you get those Char? They're the perfect match!" Diedre yelled.

"I went to the Romantic Depot off Route 9A in Elmsford – I figured Suzette's would be all out," she said as we all laughed.

"So that's why you asked me what I was gettin' Trenice," Diedre said.

"Joe would love to see me in those – I could see it now – next time he wakes my ass up early on Saturday I'ma have a pair of those on and kick him in his chest!" she hollered.

"Ouch! Damn I feel the pain just thinkin' 'bout it," I laughed.

"He likes pain – jackass would probably tell me oh yea baby - that hurt so good – do it again!" she said as we all laughed uncontrollably for about 2 minutes.

"Damn Theresa – y'all into S & M?" Rachel asked.

"I ain't into shit – Joe, on the other hand..." she said as we all laughed.

"Works for you," Carolyn said.

I reached down and picked up another box. "Wow – I almost don't wanna open it – this is some beautiful paper," I said as I kept turning the box around to admire the pink & silver wrapping with white lace bows.

"It is beautiful paper," Char said.

"I bet there's a beautiful gift inside too – but we won't ever know if Trenice doesn't ever open it," Rachel laughed.

"Oh – sorry Rachel," I laughed as I opened the box. "Oh my God – these are beautiful!" I said with tears in my eyes as I pulled out 7 silk gowns that were a perfect match to the 7 pairs of sexy sandals Char bought. "Here's to Sunday, Monday, Tuesday, Wednesday, Thursday, Friday, Saturday Love! Love, Monique," I read.

"Oh those are nice – I didn't see those at the Romantic Depot," Char said.

"I know," Monique said with a mischievous grin.

"And they didn't have those at Suzette's either!" Diedre said.

"I know that too," Monique said with a mischievous grin.

"How did you know what we were gettin' Trenice anyway?" Diedre asked.

"Oh I have my ways," Monique said with a mischievous grin.

"Where'd you get them from?" Char asked.

"I went to Victoria's Secret in the Galleria," Monique said.

"Open mine next!" Tish yelled as she grabbed her gifts and pushed them into my lap.

"Ok ok ok!" I laughed as I opened her gifts. "Ohhhh Tish.... these are beautiful!" I yelled as I held up 2 king-sized satin bed-in-a-bag sets complete with sheets, pillow cases, dust ruffles, shams, and comforters. The 1st set was deep red with gold trim and the 2nd set was powder blue with white trim.

"Wow, those are nice Tish!" Roberta yelled. "Where'd you get those?"

"I got them at Nordstrom's in the Westchester Mall," Tish beamed.

"I can't believe you remembered – thank you sooooo much!" I yelled as I squeezed her so hard she coughed.

"I guess I don't have to worry about you likin' them," she laughed.

"One of my favorites," Carlos said as he walked into the living room, pulled Diedre up into a kiss, then sat down in the chair and pulled her down onto his lap.

"Hey Beautiful," Jordan said as he plopped down on my lap. "Nice Hat," he laughed as he gave me a kiss.

"You sit here," Rachel said as she pointed to the chair next to me... "Aggghhh! Dammit you scared the hell outta me!" Rachel laughed as Jake grabbed her in a bear hug from behind and nibbled her neck and ear lobe.

"Got you good too didn't I?" he said as we all laughed.

"Hey Tee," Joe said as he came into the living room and gave Theresa a kiss before sitting next to her. "Jackass," she said. We all bust out laughing.

"What'd I do?"

"Nothing – private joke," she laughed as she started kissing him slowly and deliberately for a few minutes.

"Y'all need a room?" Char said as we all laughed.

"I'm on it," Joe said as we all laughed again.

"What's that?" Paul asked as he came into the living room, pointing at the VCR.

"Mind your business," Tish laughed as she pulled him down into the chair next to her and gave him a kiss.

While he was kissing her his eyes kept drifting towards the VCR.

"Hi everybody," Harold said as he came into the living room and sat down next to Sherrie.

"You have a good time babe?"

"Yea babe," Sherrie said as they kissed each other.

"James - whatchu doin' over there - holdin' the wall up?" Roberta said as we all laughed.

"Waitin' for you to come get me," he said seductively as he licked on a fudgesickle. Roberta made a beeline over to the doorway and we watched as the two of them licked the fudgesickle.

"Get a room!" Tim said as he walked in and we all laughed.

"Jealous?" Carolyn laughed.

"Shit I ain't jealous – if you gonna do shit in front o' me – invite me to join in or get a damn room!" he yelled as we all bust out laughing.

"Get your own damn room!" Mike yelled as he came in and we all laughed.

"Hey Mike," we all said as Wanda gave him a kiss.

I watched Khoury come in, take his shoes off, then rub his feet back and forth on the carpet. Monique got up, took off her shoes, ran over to the carpet and started rubbing her feet back and forth on the carpet too.

"What the hell are they doin'?" Jordan whispered in my ear.

"Hell if I know," I whispered back as everyone else watched. Then they leaned forward to kiss each other.

"Hi everybody," Eric said as he come into the living room. "Diana I spilled something on my pants - could you help me in the bathroom?" Eric asked.

"Sure," Diana said as she and Eric went into the bathroom.

"Dirty Diana – Oh - Dirty Diana," Tim sang as we all laughed.

"Jealous?" Carolyn said as we all laughed again.

"If you gonna do shit in front of me..."

"They already went and got a room – they got Char's bathroom!" I yelled as we all hollered.

"The food's in the kitchen y'all – hurry up and eat – Trenice wouldn't let us have any cake – she wanted y'all to see it first," Char said.

"Seen one cake – seen 'em all," Mike said as we followed the men into the kitchen.

"Awwww...." they all said as they looked at the cake.

"I haven't seen that picture in years," Jordan said.

"Your grandmother gave it to Char and Rachel to make the cake," I said.

"Look at your cute bald head!" Jake laughed.

"Look at your fat little legs," Paul laughed.

"Shit – I had a tricycle just like that when I was little," Joe said.

"Babe, Jordan and Trenice look just like Ebony and Little Harold when they were little – don't they?" Harold asked.

"Yea, they do," Sherrie said.

"Trenice you were a little cutie," James said.

"Look at the little dress Trenice has on – it matches Jordan's little shorts," Khoury laughed.

"If I didn't know better, I'd swear Trenice was tryin' to give Jordan one of them balloons," Eric laughed.

"Jordan has his head down bein' all coy too," Tim laughed.

"Shit – he wasn't bein' coy – he was gettin' his mack on," Mike laughed.

"I bet you did that with all the little girls – didn't you Jordan?" Carlos asked.

"Worked every time," Jordan laughed.

"Well this time it really paid off," Scott said.

"Awwww...." everyone said.

"It sure did," Jordan said as he pulled me into a kiss.

"Get a room!" Tim yelled as we all laughed and went back into the living room.

"Everyone get a glass!" Char yelled as she started opening bottles of champagne and filling the glasses.

"You drinkin' champagne Trenice?"

"Oh yea!" I laughed as she filled my glass along with everyone elses.

"To my best friends," she said as she raised her glass. "I love you both," she said as she took as sip of champagne.

"We love you both!" everyone yelled as we all took a sip of champagne.

"To Jordan and Trenice," Jake said as he raised his glass. "Welcome to the club – enjoy your stay!" he yelled as he took a sip of champagne.

"Welcome to the club!" everyone yelled as we all took another sip of champagne.

"To my girl Trenice," Tish said as she raised her glass. "Here's to everlasting love," she said as she took a sip of champagne.

"To everlasting love!" everyone yelled as we all took another sip of champagne.

"My man Jordan," Joe said as he raised his glass. "It's been a long time coming," he laughed as he took a sip of champagne.

"To coming a long time!" everyone yelled as we all took another sip of champagne.

"To my girl Trenice," Sherrie said as she raised her glass. "May your bed be strong enough to withstand your work outs," she laughed as she took a sip of champagne.

"May your bed be strong enough to withstand your work outs!" everyone yelled as we all took another sip of champagne.

"To my man Jordan," James said as he raised his glass. "May your marriage be strong enough and long enough to witness the day the New York Knicks **FINALLY** beat the Los Angeles Lakers in the NBA finals, win a championship, and give me the opportunity to bring your wife a newspaper with a plastic fork so she can eat her damn words!" he yelled as he took a sip of champagne.

"Oh I know we're gonna be married for at least 100 years now," Jordan laughed as he leaned over to give me a kiss and we both took a sip of champagne.

"100 years!" everyone yelled as we all took another sip of champagne.

"To my girl Trenice," Monique said as she raised her glass. "May you have all the 'Leverage,' you'll ever need," she laughed as she took a sip of champagne and winked at me.

"To **Leverage**!" everyone yelled as we all took another sip of champagne.

"What the hell is **Leverage**?" Joe asked. We all bust out laughing.

"Drink Joe – drink!" Theresa said as she pushed his glass up to his mouth and we all bust out laughing.

"What'd I say?" Joe asked as he looked around, wondering what the hell we were laughing at.

"Leverage is when you give her the power," Khoury said as we all bust out laughing.

"Well shit – gimme some more champagne so I can drink to that again!" Joe said as Char refilled his glass and we all bust out laughing.

"Then damn – I might as well give everybody some more champagne," Char said as she refilled our glasses.

"To my man Jordan," Eric said as he raised his glass. "Here's to fun in the bathroom," he laughed as he took a sip of champagne.

"To fun in the bathroom!" everyone yelled as we took another sip of champagne.

"To my man Jordan," Tim said as he raised his glass. "Here's to love and basketball!" he laughed as he took a sip of champagne.

"To love and basketball!" everyone yelled as we all took another sip of champagne.

"To my girl Trenice," Theresa said as she raised her glass. "May the flame in you burn eternally," she laughed as she took a sip of champagne.

"May the flame in you burn eternally!" everyone yelled as we all took another sip of champagne.

"To my girl Trenice," Bunny said as she raised her glass. "Here's to perfect self-expression," she laughed as she took a sip of champagne.

"You tryin' to say Trenice can't express herself clearly?" Scott asked.

"Hell no I wasn't tryin' to say that!" Bunny laughed.

"So what the hell were you tryin' to say then?" Scott laughed.

"My man — perfect self-expression is when you can tell someone how you feel or tell someone something they need to hear without hurting their feelings," Khoury said matter-of-factly.

"Go 'head wich your bad self baby," Monique said.

"Shit I thought perfect self-expression was when you said something and then you ask, 'did you understand what I said?'" Harold laughed.

"Naa man — that means she better not have to repeat herself or that's your ass," Joe said as we all bust out laughing.

"Can we drink to my toast sometime today?" Bunny laughed.

"Here's to perfect self-expression!" everyone yelled as we all took another sip of champagne.

"Perfect!" Scott yelled as we all bust out laughing again.

"To my girl Trenice," Diedre said as she raised her glass. "Here's to good health," she said as she took a sip of champagne.

"Here's to good health!" everyone yelled as we all took another sip of champagne.

"To my man Jordan," Carlos said as he raised his glass. "Here's to much wealth," he said as he took a sip of champagne.

"Here's to much wealth!" everyone yelled as we all took another sip of champagne.

"To my girl Trenice," Rachel said as she raised her glass. "Here's to spades, friends, and a clean couch!" she laughed as she took a sip of champagne and winked at me.

"To spades, friends, and a clean couch!" everyone yelled as we all took another sip of champagne.

"To my man Jordan," Paul said as he raised his glass. "May we follow in your footsteps," he said as he took a sip of champagne.

"Awww..." everyone said in unison as Paul took Tish's face in his hands, pulled her close to him, and kissed her.

"I love you so much Paul," she said with tears in her eyes.

"I love you too Tish," he said as he kissed her again.

"Get a room!" Tim yelled.

"Shut the hell up!" we all yelled in unison as we laughed and choked on champagne.

"To my man Jordan," Harold said as he raised his glass. "Here's to plenty of champagne for plenty of celebrations!" he yelled as he took a sip of champagne.

"To plenty of champagne for plenty of celebrations!" everyone yelled as we all took another sip of champagne.

"To my man Jordan," Khoury said as he raised his glass. "Here's to longevity," he said as he took a sip of champagne.

"Here's to longevity!" everyone yelled as we all took another sip of champagne.

"To my man Jordan," Scott said as he raised his glass. "Thank God you finally got it right," he said as he took a sip of champagne.

"Thank God you finally got it right!" everyone yelled as we all took another sip of champagne.

"To my man Jordan," Mike said as he raised his glass. "May you never get sick 'n tired of being sick 'n tired," he said as he shook his head and took a sip of champagne. We all looked at each other without saying anything.

"What the fuck is that supposed to mean?" Wanda yelled.

"Just what I said," Mike said.

"Oh so you tryin'a say you sick 'n tired of being sick 'n tired?"

"Why we gotta do this every time we go somewhere?" Mike yelled.

"Why you always got something smart to say every time we go somewhere?" Wanda yelled.

"I swear sometimes you get on my fuckin' nerves," Mike said as he finished his glass of champagne.

"You think you don't get on my fuckin' nerves? Huh?" Wanda yelled as she jumped up, spilling her glass of champagne on the floor.

"I'ma go y'all – congratulations," he said as he stopped to shake Jordan's hand and kiss me on the cheek before going out the door.

"Oh you wanna talk shit 'n leave right?" Wanda yelled as she went out the door behind him.

"Knock it off Wanda," Mike yelled as they went down the hall towards the elevator.

"Those two will never change," Jordan laughed.

"I'm surprised they lasted this long," Rachel laughed.

"You not mad Trenice?" Tish asked.

"Hell no - they always show their ass in public," I laughed.

"I know – just like the time we went to Tighe's Tavern," Diana laughed.

"What happened when you went to Tighe's?" Khoury asked.

"Trenice said we should go have a drink since we had to wait about ½ hour for the #3 bus so we all went across the street. We were gettin' our drink on, laughin' 'n talkin', and all of a sudden – out of nowhere – Wanda starts talkin' 'bout Mike!" Monique yelled as we all bust out laughing.

"What the hell did you say?" Khoury asked.

"We didn't say shit – we just looked at each other and then looked back at her," Diana said.

"That's Wanda for ya," Rachel laughed.

"Yo man – remember that time we all went out with Mike and the waiter brought over the steak knife?" Joe laughed.

"Hell yea!" Tim yelled. "He started yelling at the waiter talkin' 'bout, Oh I'ma stay away from you – you won't cut me," Tim laughed.

"The waiter wouldn't come back to the table for the rest of the night," Joe laughed.

"We ate, we drank, we merry – can we eat the cake now?" Char said as everyone laughed.

"Yes Char," I laughed as Mike and Wanda came back into the living room and sat down as if nothing happened.

"Just in time for cake," Jordan laughed as we all headed into the kitchen, cut the cake and went back into the living room with our plates.

"We need to get goin' – we gotta pick up the kids before mom tells us we been gone too long," Harold laughed.

"Yea – she's always tellin' us we don't know how to come back home, Sherrie laughed."

"We gotta get goin' too – Joe gotta get up for work tomorrow," Theresa said.

"You gotta work on Sundays Joe?" Jordan asked.

"I don't gotta work but since they asked me to come in they gotta pay me double-time!" Joe laughed.

"We gotta get goin' too," Scott said as he yawned and Bunny stretched.

"Good night," Carlos said as he and Diedre got up to leave.

"Good night everybody," Diedre said as they left.

"C'mon Tish," Paul said as he pulled her close to him and they walked out with their arms around each other.

"Bye everybody," Tish said as they left.

"We gonna go while we can still catch the Knick's game," Tim said as he and Carolyn got up to leave.

"Good night," Carolyn said as they left.

"Good night," James said as he and Roberta left.

"Enjoy," Diana said as she and Eric left.

"Aiiight man," Khoury said as he gave Jordan a hug and Monique gave me a hug.

"You go girl!" Monique said as they left.

"Well I guess I'll try to get up and clean this kitchen," Char said as she started to get up.

"Done!" Mike and Wanda said in unison as they both laughed.

"Thank you!" Char yelled as they left.

"Your welcome!" they yelled in unison as they headed toward the elevator.

"I don't get those two," Jake laughed.

"Nobody gets those two," Jordan laughed.

"They'll never leave each other," I laughed.

"I know that's right," Char laughed.

"They remind me of Miss Birdie and her husband," I laughed.

"Miss Birdie never remarried either," Jordan laughed.

"And she never will," Jake laughed.

"Well we might as well get going too Hun," Rachel said as she and Jake got up.

"Love to eat and run," Jake laughed.

"You ain't right," Jordan laughed as they hugged each other.

"Good night," I said as I held the door for them.

"Damn Trenice – you kickin' us out?" Jake laughed.

"Oh shut up," I said as he hugged me.

"Here Trenice," Rachel said as she handed me an envelope.

"What's this?" I asked.

"Your gift."

"Oh shit – why didn't you give it to me earlier – I could've opened it with the other gifts," I said as I started to open the envelope.

"Wait until you get home," she said as she put her hand over my hand.

"Ok then," I said as I handed Jordan the envelope and he put it in his pocket.

"Oh – one more thing," Rachel said.

"Yes?" Jordan and I asked in unison.

"Don't go on Tuesday nights," she said.

"Why can't they go on Tuesday nights?" Char asked.

"Tuesday nights are boring – it's much better on the weekend," Rachel said.

"What's much better?" Char asked.

"Mind your business," Rachel said as she winked at us.

"Oh ok," Char said as they left.

"Now I really wanna know what's in this envelope," Jordan said as he took it out his pocket.

"So open it," Char said.

"No – I don't wanna spoil the surprise – she said wait until we get home," I said.

"Well tell me what it is when you get home then," Char said as she hugged us both.

"Ok – good night Char – and thanks for everything – I love you," I said with tears in my eyes.

"I love you too – now get the hell outta here before we both start cryin'" she said as she started pushing us out the door.

"Not so fast Char," Jordan said as he ran into the living room, popped the tape out of the camcorder, put it in his jacket, and came back to the door.

"Shit – I almost had it!" Char laughed.

"Almost doesn't count," he said as he gave Char a peck on the cheek on his way out the door and she stood in the doorway, watching us until we got in the elevator.

I thought I heard banging on the door, but I wasn't getting up to answer it – and neither was he...

"Well hurry up – we haven't got all damn day!" we heard.

"Who is that?" he breathed.

"It's Char and Carl," I said.

"What are they doing here?" he asked.

"We're getting married today," I said.

"Yes we are," he said.

"Are y'all coming?" Char yelled.

"Yeeeessssss!" Jordan yelled.

"Good morning," Carl said as he stood in the doorway of our bedroom.

"Carl – what the fuck are you doing in here?" Jordan yelled as he jumped up off me and pulled up the sheet around us.

"Good morning y'all, Char said as she pushed past Carl, came into the bedroom, and sat on our bed.

"Excuse me! Do you mind?" Jordan yelled. I bust out laughing. Carl and Char looked at each other and bust out laughing. "What's so damn funny?" Jordan yelled.

"We didn't answer the door!" I laughed while holding my stomach.

"So they just let themselves in?" Jordan yelled. We all continued to laugh but Jordan wasn't the least bit amused.

"Now you know how it feels man," Carl laughed. Jordan began to laugh too.

"Oh – so that's what this is about?" Jordan laughed.

"Yea man!" Carl laughed.

"You lucky we love y'all or you would'a never got away with that shit," Jordan laughed.

"Okay guys – y'all getting' married today and I have a lot to help Trenice with – get up!" she yelled as she tried to snatch the sheet off of us...

"Oh hell no!" Jordan laughed as he held on to the sheet. "We're not getting up until y'all get out!"

"Okay – you got sixty seconds – I'm coming back whether you're ready or not," Char laughed.

"Bye y'all," Carl laughed as he left the bedroom.

"Y'all got 20 seconds left," Char yelled as we jumped outta bed and threw on our robes before Char came back into the bedroom. "Okay Trenice – into the shower you go – we gotta get moving!" Char said as she pushed me towards the shower.

"Let's go Jordan," Jake said as he took Jordan by one arm, Carl took Jordan by the other arm, and they both pushed him towards the other bathroom. We hadn't realized that Jake and Rachel were already in the house.

"Hey Trenice," Rachel said as she came into the bedroom and sat on our bed.

"She's in the shower," Char said as I turned on the water, grabbed the body wash, and commenced to the job at hand. I laughed to myself as I heard Char telling Rachel how they had to come into the bedroom to get us up because we refused to answer the door.

"They kept saying they were coming," Char laughed.

"Why am I not surprised," Rachel laughed as I came into the bedroom from the shower. My clothes were already laid out on the bed and pressed. I started to cry uncontrollably.

"Girl, what's wrong?" Char said as she pulled me to her, grabbed me into a hug, and placed my head on her shoulder.

"You okay Trenice?" Rachel asked as she came up behind me and started rubbing my back.

"I love y'all so much," I sniffed as I grabbed them both and pulled them into a hug. We all bust out laughing as my towel dropped.

"Girl, get dressed!" Char laughed as she opened my panties and motioned with her hand, commanding me to step into them.

"Girl, hold still," Rachel laughed as she extended my arms, put my bra straps on my shoulders, and hooked my bra in the back. As they waited for me to finish getting dressed, we had no idea what was transpiring in the other room...

"Jordan you done yet?" Jake yelled.

"I'm shaving," Jordan answered.

"Well hurry up!" Carl yelled back.

"Don't cut yourself – you need to look good for your wedding," Jake said.

"Alright y'all – we'll see you later," Char said as she and Rachel made sure I went out the door without taking a detour to go say good bye to Jordan. After we left, they continued their conversation...

"Can I ask y'all something?" Carl asked as Jordan started getting dressed.

"Sure Carl," Jake answered. "What's up?"

"It's personal," Carl said.

"What's wrong Carl?" Jordan asked.

"I don't know how to ask," Carl said.

"Just say it man," Jake said.

"Okay... here goes... never mind," Carl said.

"Carl?" Jordan asked as he sat down on the bed and motioned for Carl to sit next to him.

"Yes Jordan?" Carl answered.

"After everything we've been through since we've met you, I feel like you're my brother," Jordan said as he put his hand on Carl's shoulder.

"Thanks Jordan – that means a lot," Carl said.

"I'm getting married today," Jordan said.

"I know Jordan," Carl said.

"You're going to share in the happiest day of my life," Jordan said. "Besides Jake, no one else could come up in my house, kick me outta my own bedroom, and push me into the shower so say what the fuck you gotta say," Jordan laughed.

"Okay," Carl said as he put his head down.

"What's wrong man?" Jake asked with concern.

"It's Char... or maybe it's me," Carl said.

"Okay," Jordan said.

"Lately she's been very quiet," Carl said.

"That's unusual for Char," Jordan said.

"That's what's bothering you man?" Jordan asked.

"See — I should'a never said anything," Carl said.

"Carl, my brother, you gotta learn how to read your woman," Jake said.

"Whatchu mean?" Carl asked.

"You have nothing to worry about," Jordan said.

"Thanks y'all," Carl said. I feel so stupid.

"No need to feel stupid brother," Jordan said. "How are you supposed to know if no one tells you?"

"Exactly," Jake agreed.

"Let's get going — I got things to do," Jordan laughed as they followed him out into the hallway and the door slammed shut behind them.

"I was just getting ready to call you," Bernadette said as we flew in the door.

"Hey Bernadette," I breathed as we sat down in our massage chairs.

"Y'all want the Deluxe Pedicure or the SPA Pedicure?" her assistant asked.

"Give 'em the SPA Pedicure," Bernadette answered for us.

"Oooohhh... This feels nice..." Char said as she slumped down in the chair.

"It sure does," Rachel said as the technicians got to work on our pedicures.

"Everything okay Trenice?" Bernadette asked.

"Yes Bernadette," I answered.

"Okay – if you need anything just ask." We all bust out laughing. Bernadette turned around and gave us a look. "What's so funny?" she asked.

"Nothing – private joke," I laughed.

"Well let a sista in," she said.

"I hope the guys are okay and on schedule," Char said, changing the subject.

"If Jordan has anything to say about it, they're ahead of schedule," I said as I smiled at Char. I can always count on her to read my mind.

"So how are you and Carl?" Rachel asked.

"We're great...," Char sighed.

"I'm so happy for you Char," I said.

"It's not her business," Char said while pointing towards the technician working on my feet.

"Okay then!" Rachel laughed.

"You like?" the technician asked as I sat there looking at my toes.

"Hmmm...," I said as I continued looking at my toes without getting up.

"Is everything okay Trenice?" Bernadette asked as she came over.

"I love this color," I sighed. "What's the name of it?"

"I Do," Bernadette answered.

"Aww....," we said in unison.

"What's the name of the top coat?" I asked as we all sat down to dry our toes.

"Drink your champagne ladies," Bernadette ordered. Char and Rachel started drinking their champagne right away but I didn't pick up my glass.

"Girl, you ain't drinkin?" Char asked.

"Champagne goes straight to my head," I answered.

"One glass won't hurt Trenice – drink up," Rachel said as she picked up my glass and handed it to me.

"Yes Maam," I said as I started drinking. "Bernadette?"

"Yes Trenice?"

"What's the name of the top coat?" I asked again as the technicians started working on our nails...

"Slippery When Wet," Bernadette answered. That did it...

"AAAAHHHHHHHH...

HA, HA, HA, HA, HA, HA, HA, HA, HA, HA, HA, HA, HA, HA, HA, HA, HA, HA, HA, HA... AAAAHHHHHHHHH...

HA, HA, HA, HA, HA, HA, HA, HA, HA, HA, HA, HA, HA, HA, HA, HA, HA, HA, HA, HA... AAAAHHHHHHHHH...

HA, HA, HA, HA, HA, HA, HA, HA, HA, HA, HA, HA, HA, HA, HA, HA, HA, HA, HA, HA... AAAAHHHHHHHHH...

HA, HA, HA, HA, HA, HA, HA, HA, HA, HA, HA,
HA, HA, HA, HA, HA, HA, HA, HA, HA...
AAAAHHHHHHHH...
HA, HA, HA, HA, HA, HA, HA, HA, HA, HA, HA,
HA, HA, HA, HA, HA, HA, HA, HA, HA..."

"Jordan!" Mr. Giovanni exclaimed when they walked in.

"Hello Mr. Giovanni – this is Jake and Carl," Jordan said as he introduced them.

"Right this way gentlemen," Mr. Giovanni said as he directed them to the dressing room. "You guys get undressed – I'll be right back," Mr. Giovanni said.

"Arms out at your sides please," Raul said as he approached Carl.

"Why? Am I being searched?" Carl laughed.

"Arms out at your sides please," Raul repeated.

"Why?" Carl asked again.

"Is there a problem?" Mr. Giovanni asked as he brought in the tuxedos, shirts, ties, shirts, and shoes.

"Monsieur doesn't want to extend his arms," Raul answered.

"I just want to know why," Carl said.

"Raul, answer the client's question," Mr. Giovanni commanded.

"Sir, please extend your arms so I can make sure the sleeves are the right length," Raul explained.

"That's all you had to say man," Carl said as he extended his arms.

"My apologies Monsieur," Raul said as he took the measurements. "Spread your legs," Raul commanded.

"Wait a damn minute!" Carl yelled as he jumped back. Jordan and Jake bust out laughing.

"My apologies Monsieur – I need to measure the length of your inseam from your crotch to the bottom of your leg," Raul said as he proceeded to take the measurement...

"You ain't gotta touch my balls man!" Carl yelled.

"Damn Carl – Relax!" Jordan laughed.

"I'm very sorry Monsieur – I don't mean to make you uncomfortable – please don't tell Mr. Giovanni," Raul pleaded, "He fire me for upsetting the clients..."

What's going on here?" Mr. Giovanni asked as he came back into the dressing room. "Raul – why aren't they dressed?"

"I finish taking measurements," Raul answered.

"Okay then – gentlemen get dressed so we can make sure everything fits – I'll be back in a few minutes – Raul please come assist these customers in the front," Mr. Giovanni

commanded as he snapped his finger and Raul
followed him out the dressing room.

"Damn – Giovanni doesn't play does he?"
Carl laughed.

"No he doesn't – and he shouldn't," Jordan
answered as they continued getting dressed.

"I'm surprised you went with the Stamford
shoes," Jake said as he slipped them on.

"Damn – we look good," Carl said as he
stood in the mirror.

"We sure do," Jordan said as Jake stood on
the left side and Joran stood on the right.

"I'm glad you went with the Stamford
shoes Jordan – I could dance all night in these,"
Carl said.

"I know," Jordan laughed.

"Ahhh yes – turn around – le'me see," Mr.
Giovanni said as he came into the dressing room.
"Raul – give me your phone," he commanded as
Raul gave Mr. Giovanni his cell phone and Mr.
Giovanni took a picture of them. "You are happy
– yes?" Mr. Giovanni asked.

"Very," Jordan answered.

"Raul – make sure they have everything
they need – gentlemen, your bags will be at the
front when you come out," he said as he left the
dressing room.

"Your clothes please," Raul said as he took
the tuxedos, bagged them, then took the shirts,
the ties, the shoes, and bagged them separately
for Carl, Jordan, and Jake.

"What's he going to do with the picture?" Carl asked as they were preparing to leave the store.

"He's going to frame it and put it right there," Jake answered as he pointed to the client wall.

"Oh wow – look at all his clients," Carl said.

"Let's go – my future wife is waiting," Jordan said.

"Congratulations – and thank you for your business," Mr. Giovanni said as they left.

When we got to David's Bridal my mother, grandmother, Miss April, and Miss June were waiting for us.

"'Bout damn time!" Grandma said. As soon as we got inside, they wasted no time.

"Right this way Ms. Roberts – everything's ready, Jessica said as she directed us towards the dressing rooms.

"Okay ladies – let's get you into these dresses," Jessica said as she started to help everyone out of their clothes.

"Mom... your dress is beautiful," I sighed when I saw her gown. The Champagne Pearl Jeweled Necklace Halter Mesh Gown was perfect. I couldn't stop the tears.

"Oh my God Trenice – knock it off," my mother laughed.

"I can't help it... you look so beautiful..."

"You do look beautiful Claire," Grandma said.

"Whatchu tryin'a say?" Miss June said as she stepped out in her Sleeveless Mesh Metallic Dress with Corded Lace.

"Aww shit!" we all said in unison as she modeled for us.

"Go 'head Miss Gladys!" Char yelled when my grandmother came out wearing the Three Piece Beaded Chiffon Pant Suit.

"Work it Ma!" my mother shouted as Grandma took off the jacket, placed her hand on her hip, paused, turned, and showed us her sequined back.

"She ain't got shit on me," Miss April said as she strutted to the mirror in her Two Piece Lace and Jersey Pant Suit.

"Yes Honey!" Rachel shouted as Miss April showed off the iridescent sequins and lace accents on the shoulder and jacket cuffs.

"Okay ladies," Jessica said as she took Char and Rachel into the 2nd dressing room. We were all speechless when they returned wearing their One Shoulder Dress with Crepe Bodice featuring a Satin Sash at the waist. The Long Soft Matte Charmeuse Skirt with Side Slit flowed with ease as the girls came to the stage, put their hands on their hips, and showed us their legs.

"Woo hoo!" my mom shouted.

"Legs for days!" Miss June laughed.

"You ready Trenice?" Jessica asked.

"I'm ready," I answered as I followed her into the 2nd dressing room. I wasn't ready for what happened when I came out...

"Trenice! You look beautiful! Is that your dress?" Sissy announced to the entire store.

"Thank you Sissy – yes, this is my dress," I answered through a phony smile.

"Is Trudy here?" she asked.

"She's not with you?" I asked, dreading the answer.

"Chile, I ain't seen Trudy in weeks," she answered.

"Thank God," I mumbled.

"What?" Sissy asked.

"Oh – I said thank God the dress fits perfect – have a nice day!" I yelled as I darted back into the dressing room with Jessica.

"What the fuck she doing here?" Char asked.

"Look at my princess," my mother whispered with tears in her eyes

"Knock it off Claire," Grandma said with tears in her eyes.

"Oh hush Ma," my mother said.

"You look beautiful Trenice," Char said.

"This design is one of my favorites," Rachel said as she admired the petite Strapless Tulle Ball Gown with Satin Bodice. I stood still as they all admired the Strapless Satin Bodice accented with intricate beaded metallic embroidery and an elegant lace-up back.

"I've never seen a more beautiful model for this dress Trenice, Jessica said.

"Thank you," I said.

"Let me go get the Tiara and your shoes," Jessica said as she left to go get them. "Here – try this one," Jessica said as she handed me the Heavily Beaded Crystal Tiara.

"Oooohhh...," they all said in unison when I tried it on.

"It's perfect," I said as I handed it to Char.

"Okay ladies – let's make sure the shoes fit so Trenice isn't late for her big day," Jessica said as she handed us our shoes.

"Ohhh... I like these!" Rachel said as she put them on.

"Ohhh... these are comfortable," Miss April said.

"And wide width too – finally a shoe I can wear," Miss June laughed.

"Char, please give Trenice the Tiara – then I need everyone to get together for a picture," Jessica said as she grabbed her cell phone. "No tears Trenice," she said as she took a few pictures. "Okay ladies – I'll meet you up front," she said as she helped us all out of our clothes, bagged them, and re-boxed our shoes. After we all got dressed and started to leave the dressing room, I stopped to give Jessica a hug and started to cry.

"Thank you sooo much...," I sniffed.

"You're welcome Trenice – guess what?"

"What?" I asked as I wiped my eyes.

"Rachel's been in here a few times trying on wedding dresses – but you didn't get that from me," she whispered in my ear and then ran to the front of the store.

"Okay y'all – I'm going to make sure Trenice gets to Greg's – we'll meet you back at the house – c'mon Trenice," Char said as we jumped in her car and took off...

"Hi guys," Tyler said as they entered the lobby.

"Damn man – you kinda early," Carl laughed.

"He's right on time," Jordan said as they all headed towards the elevator.

"You want me to wait downstairs?" Tyler asked as they got off the elevator.

"No Tyler – you good – you can wait in the living room while we get ready," Jordan said.

"Trenice is one lucky woman," Tyler said.

"I'm the lucky one," Jordan said.

"We'll go inside and start getting dressed – c'mon Carl," Jake said as they started down the hallway towards the guest room. Jordan started down the hall but was interrupted by a knock on the door...

"Who is it?" Jordan asked.

"Yonkers Police."

"I got this," Tyler said as he opened the door. "May we help you officers?" Tyler asked.

"May we come in?" The officer asked.

"For what?" Jordan asked.

"Are you Jordan Williams?" the officer asked.

"Yes he is – and I'm his attorney – what can we do for you?" Tyler asked as he stepped in front of Jordan.

"We need to ask you a few questions," the officer answered as they both stepped inside.

"I never said you could come in," Jordan laughed.

"I'm Detective Rosa and this is Detective Morack," he said. May we sit down?"

"Now's not a good time – what's this about – c'mon sit down," Jordan said as Tyler and the detectives followed him into the living room.

"We're looking into Dr. Aiden's death and we need to ask you some questions," Detective Rosa said.

"Dr. Aiden?" Carl asked. Jordan turned around and saw Carl and Jake standing in the living room.

"Why the hell do you need to ask me questions?" Jordan yelled. "He wasn't my damn doctor!"

"Because we have reason to believe you were the last one to see him alive," Detective Morack answered.

"Not another word Jordan," Tyler said as he stood up.

"Oh I have a few words for them!" Jordan snapped, "Mutha fucka's comin' up in here on my wedding day with this bullshit – get the fuck outta my house!"

"I'm sorry you're upset, but we need to get to the bottom of this," Detective Rosa said...

"My client has asked you to leave," Tyler said as he stood between Jordan and the detectives. "I'll be happy to schedule a time when we can meet and answer any questions you have," Tyler said as he handed them both his business card. The detectives stood there for a few moments as if they didn't understand what Tyler said. Jordan opened the front door and stood there. "This way detectives," Tyler said as he led them towards the door.

"See you soon," Detective Rosa said eerily as he passed Jordan. Jordan slammed the door.

"Damn – what was that all about?" Carl asked.

"I don't know and I don't care – my wife is waiting and I'm not going to be late – let's go guys!" Jordan said as he went down the hall and Carl and Jake followed. "Tyler if anybody else comes to my door with some bullshit..."

"I got it Jordan – get dressed," Tyler laughed.

"What the fuck was she doing there?" Char asked.

"Who?" I answered, pretending I forgot...

"Sissy!" Char yelled.

"Hell if I know," I laughed.

"Was Trudy with her?"

"No girl – she said she hasn't seen Trudy in weeks!"

"I wonder why?"

"I don't know and I don't care – I'm glad she wasn't here though," I laughed. When we pulled up to the salon, Greg wasted no time.

"Hi Trenice – c'mon in – I gotta get you outta here on time," he said as he opened the car door.

"I need to park the car," Char said.

"Leave it here – I'll keep an eye on it," Greg said as we went inside and sat in the shampoo chairs.

"Girl, you ain't neva lie!" Char exclaimed as Greg massaged her scalp.

"I told you he has magic hands," I said as he came over to massage my scalp.

"Thank you ladies," he said as he rinsed my hair, then Char's.

"And he does it while he shampoos your hair so you don't spend all day here too – not that I would mind," Char laughed.

"Okay ladies – time for your conditioner," Greg said as he conditioned Char's hair, then mine.

"Oochhh... this smells nice," I said.

"I'll be back in two minutes," Greg said as he went to answer the phone.

"You ready for today Trenice?" Char asked.

"Yea...," I sighed.

"I think I'm ready too," Char said.

"I know Char."

"I think I'm ready to get married," Char said.

"Oh my God! Oh my God!" I started screaming...

"What's wrong?" Greg said as he came running towards us.

"Nothing — Trenice just crazy," Char laughed.

"Well let me rinse you out and get you under the dryer," Greg said as he rinsed Char's hair then mine. "This way ladies," he said as he led us to the styling chairs. "Trenice, you want a roll with cascading curls down the front right?"

"Yes Greg," I answered.

"Char, you want a side part and straight right?"

"Yes Greg," she answered.

"Okay — would you like me to use a flat iron?"

"Yes Greg," Char answered.

"Okay — I'll put you both under the dryer, then I'll do you first, then Trenice," he said.

"Why don't you do Trenice first?" Char asked.

"I always save the best for last," Greg said with a wink as he went back to the front of the salon.

"I'm gonna ask him to marry me," Char said.

"I know Char."

"How you know Trenice?"

"After you finally got over Cornell you told me the next man you meet you're gonna ask him to marry you."

"You remembered!" Char exclaimed.

"Of course," I answered.

"Okay Char – I'm ready for you," Greg said as he took her from under the dryer. I stayed under the dryer and watched as Greg worked. You could tell he took pride in his work because he would stop, look at your hair, shake his head if it wasn't quite right, or smile if it was just right. "How do you like it?" he asked Char as she spun in the chair from left to right.

"I love it Greg," she sighed.

"Did you bring the tiara for Trenice?"

"Yea – it's in the car – I'll get it," Char said as she went to the car.

"Something's different about her," he said as he started working on my hair.

"She's happy," I said.

"Yes she is," he said as Char came in with the tiara.

"I got a ticket," Char said.

"I'll take care of it," Greg said, matter-of-factly.

"You will?" Char asked.

"Yes Char – Trenice do you want to sit back under the dryer with gel or do you want hair spray?"

"I want hair spray," I answered.

"Okay then – pass me the tiara Char – I'm glad you don't want the gel Trenice – you have soft hair and the gel will break it," Greg said as he continued to work on my hair. "Do you want oil sheen?"

"Yes Greg," I answered.

"Since we're just using oil sheen, when you go to take your hair down you won't have any problems – your curls will hold until tomorrow – how do you like it?" he asked as he spun me around.

"I love it!" I exclaimed.

"Thank you Trenice – congratulations – Char, make sure you leave your ticket with me so I can take care of it."

"Thank you Greg," we both said in unison.

"You're welcome – see you after the wedding."

"Oooohhh… this is nice!" I exclaimed when Vanessa opened the door.

"Uh, Uh, Uh – that way ladies," Vanessa said as she pushed us towards the master bedroom.

"Okay, okay!" Char laughed as we headed into the bedroom.

"You look beautiful Trenice," Grandma said with tears in her eyes.

"Everybody's dressed but you two – c'mon Char," Rachel said as she took Rachel by the arm and walked her out the master bedroom and into the guest room.

"Who's gonna help Trenice get ready?" Char asked.

"I got her," Mom said as she took me by the arm. "Stop laughing Trenice," she said as she helped me step into my dress.

"I can't help it – you're tickling me!" I laughed.

"Oooohhhhh Trenice – you look pretty!" Shaliyah said as she burst into the bedroom...

"Shaliyah! Get out!" Mom yelled.

"It's alright Ma – she can help," I said.

"She's not supposed to be in here Trenice," Mom said.

"I just wanted to see Trenice," Shaliyah said with tears in her eyes.

"Oh no you don't – not on my wedding day," I said as I gave her a big, loud smooch on her cheek. "I really need your help Shaliyah."

"You do Trenice?" she perked.

"Yes," I answered.

"Okay! What can I do?" she asked.

"I need you to make sure everyone sits where they're supposed to when they come in – and nobody can come to the bedrooms okay?" I asked her.

"Okay!" Shaliyah exclaimed with a smile as she skipped down the hall.

"That's her problem now – she gets around you and thinks she doesn't have to listen," Mom said.

"That's because she knows she doesn't have too," I laughed.

"Well let her ass come stay with you then," Mom said.

"No thank you," I laughed.

"Exactly," Mom said.

"Hello Reverend," I heard my grandmother say.

"Hello everyone," Reverend Bruce said as he came in. "Is everyone ready?"

"I'm ready," Jordan answered.

"I know that's right!" Miss June said as everyone else erupted in laughter.

"Alrighty then," Reverend Bruce said as I began to hear the piano.

"It's time Trenice," my mother said as she began walking me down the hall towards the living room. When I turned the corner, I was in awe. My brothers and sisters were on one sectional to the right, our friends were on the other sectional to the left, and Jordan was sitting on the bench, playing the piano. Jake and Carl were standing to the left of the piano, the Reverend, Miss April, and Miss June were in the middle, and my grandmother, Char, and Rachel were standing to the right. The women looked exquisite in their suits and gowns and the men were sexy as hell in their Black Celebration Tuxedos by David Tutera. The White Fitted Vince turn Down Collar shirt along with the Larr Brio Simply Solid Matching Long Tie made them all a sensual sight for sore eyes from the top of their smooth, clear shaven faces to the soles of their Frederico Leone Black Matte Stanford Shoes... and mine was the sexiest of them all. I started crying as soon as I recognized the song Jordan was playing. My mother walked me towards the piano and stood beside my grandmother as Jordan extended his hand to take mine and I sat down beside him on the bench. Jordan began singing with Jake and Carl singing in the background...

Let Me Put Some Love In Your Life

VS I   Dry your eyes, baby don't cry, 'cause I'm here. I'll take away your hurt, and pain, and fear.

VS II   Come and feel my warm embrace. Your sweet love I won't waste. I hope this offer you will take. Baby, please don't hesitate.

CHORUS Let me put some love in your life. I will turn your gray skies blue. Let me put some love in your life.

I will give you a love that's true.

VS III   I'll be around, I won't let you down,
if you need me. I'll be right there for
you my dear — that's a guarantee.

VS IV   I promise you a life of love and
laughter. They'll be so many
mornings after. All you have to do is
just concede. Let it happen, just let
it be.

Repeat Chorus

Let me... Let me Baby...

Tears flowed down his cheeks as he took my face
in his hands and kissed my tears. Shaliyah was
on duty making sure everyone had tissues,
including Reverend Bruce. After Shaliyah
collected the tissues from everyone she placed our
'Tears of Joy' basket on the living room table and
ran up to take her place in front of Mom. Jordan
and I stood in front of Reverend Bruce as he took
out the vows we chose from MyWeddingVows.com
and began with Holding Hands...

*"Trenice please face Jordan and hold his
hands, palms up, so you may see the gift that
they are to you.*

*These are the hands of your best friend, young
and strong and vibrant with love, that are
holding yours on your wedding day, as he
promises to love you all the days of his life.*

*These are the hands that will work along side
yours, as together you build your future, as you
laugh and cry, as you share your innermost
secrets and dreams.*

*These are the hands you will place with
expectant joy against your stomach, until he too,
feels his child stir within you.*

*These are the hands that look so large and
strong, yet will be so gentle as he holds your baby
for the first time.*

*These are the hands that will work long hours for
you and your new family.*

*These are that hands that will passionately love
you and cherish you through the years, for a
lifetime of happiness.*

*These are the hands that will countless times
wipe the tears from your eyes: tears of sorrow
and tears of joy.*

These are the hands that will comfort you in illness, and hold you when fear or grief wrack your mind.

These are the hands that will tenderly lift your chin and brush your cheek as they raise your face to look into his eyes: eyes that are filled completely with his overwhelming love and desire for you."

I took Jordan's left hand and placed it on my stomach. Shaliyah was on duty again, making sure everyone had tissues, then collecting them and placing the 'Tears of Joy' basket back on the table. Reverend Bruce waited for her to take her place again before he continued...

"Jordan, please hold Trenice's hands, palms up, where you may see the gift that they are to you.

These are the hands of your best friend, smooth, young and carefree, that are holding yours on your wedding day, as she pledges her love and commitment to you all the days of her life.

These are the hands that will hold each child in tender love, soothing them through illness and hurt, supporting and encouraging them along the way, and knowing when it is time to let go.

These are the hands that will massage tension from your neck and back in the evenings after you've both had a long hard day.

These are the hands that will hold you tight as you struggle through difficult times.

These are the hands that will comfort you when you are sick, or console you when you are grieving.

These are the hands that will passionately love you and cherish you through the years, for a lifetime of happiness.

These are the hands that will hold you in joy and excitement and hope, each time she tells you that you are to have another child, that together you have created a new life.

These are the hands that will give you support as she encourages you to chase down your dreams. Together as a team, everything you wish for can be realized.

Lord, bless these hands that you see before you this day. May they always be held by one another. Give them the strength to hold on during the storms of stress and the dark of disillusionment. Keep them tender and gentle as they nurture each other in their wondrous love.

*Help these hands to continue building a
relationship founded in your grace, rich in caring,
and devoted in reaching for your perfection.
May Jordan and Trenice see their four hands as
healer, protector, shelter and guide. We ask this
in Jesus name, Amen."*

"Amen!" everyone said in unison as
Shaliyah was back on duty, making sure
everyone had tissues, collecting the tissues,
placing our 'Tears of Joy' basket back on the
table, and taking her place in front of Mom.
Reverend Bruce continued with the Questions of
Intention and Exchange of Vows...

*"Will you please, as an expression that
your hearts are joined together in love, now face
each other and join your hands.*

*Jordan, do you take Trenice to be your
wedded wife, to live together in marriage? Do you
promise to love her, comfort her, honor and keep
her for better or worse, for richer or poorer, in
sickness and in health, and forsaking all others,
be faithful only to her, so long as you both shall
live?"*

"I do," Jordan answered.

"Then tell her," Reverend Bruce said.

"I, Jordan, take you, Trenice, to be my wife, my partner in life and my one true love. I will cherish our friendship and love you today, tomorrow, and forever. I will trust you and honor you. I will laugh with you and cry with you. I will love you faithfully through the best and the worst, through the difficult, and the easy. No matter what may come I will always be there. As I have given you my hand to hold, so I give you my life to keep, so help me God."

"Trenice, do you take Jordan to be your wedded husband to live together in marriage? Do you promise to love him, comfort him, honor and keep him for better or worse, for richer or poorer, in sickness and in health and forsaking all others, be faithful only to him, so long as you both shall live?"

"I do," I answered.

"Then tell him," Reverend Bruce said.

"I, Trenice, take you, Jordan, to be my husband, my partner in life and my one true love. I will cherish our friendship and love you today, tomorrow, and forever. I will trust you and honor you. I will laugh with you and cry with you. I will love you faithfully through the best and the worst, through the difficult, and the easy. No matter what may come I will always be there. As

I have given you my hand to hold, so I give you my life to keep, so help me God."

"May I have the rings?" Reverend Bruce asked. Jordan looked to Carl as he took the 14K White Gold Trio set out his pocket. The engagement ring had 23 diamonds with a total diamond weight of 2/3 cts. The wedding band had 11 diamonds with a total diamond weight of 1/5 cts. The men's wedding band had 33 diamonds with a total diamond weight of 2/3 cts. As Carl handed the rings to Reverend Bruce he laughed and said, "There's enough diamonds here to make you go blind!" Everyone erupted in laughter. Reverend Bruce waited for everyone to settle down before he continued with the Blessing of the Rings...

"The wedding ring is the outward and visible sign of an inward and spiritual bond which unites two loyal hearts in endless love. It is a seal of the vows Jordan and Trenice have made to one another. Lord, bless these rings that Jordan and Trenice, who give them, and who wear them, may ever abide in thy peace, living together in unity, love and happiness for the rest of their lives. Jordan, Trenice, please exchange your rings."

Jordan took the engagement ring and the wedding band from Reverend Bruce, took my left hand, placed the rings on my ring finger, and repeated after Reverend Bruce: "Trenice, I give you this ring as a symbol of our vows, and with all that I am, and all that I have, I honor you. In the name of the Father, the Son, and the Holy Spirit, with this ring, I thee wed."

I took the wedding band from Reverend Bruce, took Jordan's left hand, placed the ring on his ring finger, and repeated after Reverend Bruce: "Jordan, I give you this ring as a symbol of our vows, and with all that I am, and all that I have, I honor you. In the name of the Father, the Son, and the Holy Spirit, with this ring, I thee wed."

Reverend Bruce finished up with the Declaration of Marriage...

"In as much as you have each pledged to the other your lifelong commitment, love, and devotion, I now pronounce you husband and wife, in the name of the Father, the Son, and the Holy Spirit! Those whom God has joined together let no one put asunder! Jordan, you may kiss your bride!"

Reception

"It is my pleasure to introduce to you Mr. & Mrs. Jordan Williams!" Reverend Bruce announced as we kissed.

"Y'all can stop now," Char said as everyone erupted in laughter. It didn't matter to us one bit. We stayed locked in our embrace and continued kissing until we felt like stopping and when we did stop, we still didn't let go of each other.

"Move Ma," my mother said as she pushed Grandma out of the way to get to us first. "I'm so happy for you," my mother said as she grabbed us both into a hug.

"Me to Claire — but I can't breathe," Jordan said as everyone erupted in laughter again.

"Let 'em go Claire," Miss June said as she pulled my mother away from us so she could grab us into a hug. "You finally got it right," she said as she hugged us both.

"Yes I did Mum Mum," Jordan agreed.

"Alright, Alright, — let somebody else get in there," Grandma laughed as she pushed her way towards us to embrace us.

"Don't be so greedy Gladys," Miss April said as she embraced us along with Grandma. The four of us stood there hugging for a few moments until Magic started playing, 'You're My First, Your My Last, My Everything!' Everyone watched as we danced and the entire room erupted in applause after the song was over.

"We finally got it together Beautiful," Jordan whispered in my ear as he pulled me close.

"Yes we did," I whispered back.

"Get a room!" Tim yelled as the room erupted in laughter. Jordan took me by the hand and led me across the floor to our table. Everyone else followed and sat down at their tables. Each table was decorated in powder blue and white, with red roses in the center. The staff at the Riverview on Warburton Avenue in Hastings really outdid themselves. For a moment, I forgot I was in our penthouse.

"I wanna sit with Trenice!" Shaliyah yelled as she ran to our table and sat down.

Before my mother could say a word, I said, "Shaliyah, your table is over there," as I pointed to the table with the Bridal Party sign.

"I get to sit there?" she squealed.

"Yes Shaliyah," I answered with a kiss on her cheek. She beamed as Char, Carl, Jake, Rachel, Mom, Grandma, Miss April, and Miss June joined her and Reverend Bruce. My brothers and sisters sat at the table in the middle of the room. Tish, Paul, Theresa, Joe, Monique, Khoury, Roberta, James, Diana, and Eric sat at the table to the left and Carolyn, Tim, Sherrie, Harold, Diedre, Carlos, Wanda, Mike, Bunny, and Scott sat at the table to the right.

The Diamond Cocktail Hour started with Coconut Shrimp, Clams Oreganato, Salmon Mousse on Endive, Coconut Chicken, Bacon Wrapped Scallops, Chicken Kabobs with Pineapple, Swedish Meatballs, Imported & Domestic Cheese, Assorted Crackers, and Assorted Pastry Puffs and Magic started playing, 'Who Do You Love,' by Bernard White.

As the staff began pouring champagne, my mother was quick to snatch Shaliyah's glass from her. "You can't have that!" she snapped.

"Madame, that's ginger ale," the server said.

"Oh, okay," Mom laughed.

Everyone got their glasses and the toasting began with Shaliyah. "Excuse me everybody," she squealed as she clanged her glass. When we all gave her our attention she said, "Congratulations Trenice and Jordan – and I love my new big brother!" Awww… everyone said in unison as Shaliyah ran to Jordan, grabbed him around the neck, kissed him on the cheek, and ran back to the table. I smiled to myself as the photographer caught the kiss.

We continued to sit, eat, and drink as the toasts continued with my brothers and sisters, starting with Marlowe. "Congratulations to you both – let me know when I can move in," he said as the room erupted in laughter.

"Le'me git a couple o' dollars," Chandler said.

"Le'me come watch cable," Thelma said.

"I need to use your computer," Sheila said.

"I need to borrow your car… when you finally get one," Tina laughed.

"Make sure you keep Hennessey on deck for me," Troy said.

"I'll always be your D.J.," Smalls said.

"Le'me borrow your books – I might not bring them back – but le'me borrow them anyway," Keisha laughed.

"Le'me use your phone – mine won't be back on 'till next month," Wayne laughed.

"Le'me know whatchall cookin' tomorrow," Michelle laughed.

Char stood up to toast as Magic started playing, 'Lovely Day,' by Bill Withers. The servers went around the room to make sure everyone had more champagne but when they came to our table I said, "No thank you," before he could refill my glass.

"Madam, it's your wedding day," the server said as he took my glass and refilled it.

"I'd like some ginger ale please," I said as if he asked me what I'd like.

"As you wish," the server said as he motioned for another server to bring over a pitcher of ginger ale. "Would you like some ginger ale as well Monsieur?" the server asked Jordan.

"Yes please," Jordan answered as the server poured Jordan some ginger ale. Char started crying and Carl stood up to comfort her.

"What's wrong?" Carl asked as he pulled Char close to him.

"Nothing," Char answered. "Trenice, I love you with all my heart," she said as she continued to cry.

"I love you too Char," I said as I started tearing up.

"You're the sister I always wanted," she said as she left the table to come give me a hug.

"Aww... everyone said in unison as I stood up from the table to receive her hug and hug her back. Shaliyah jumped up from the table to run and get the box of tissues and our 'Tears of Joy' basket as we hugged each other and cried.

"I'm so happy for you Trenice," Char said.

"Thank you Char," I said. Shaliyah stood there patiently waiting for us to dry our eyes with the tissues and put them in the 'Tears of Joy' basket. When we were done, Shaliyah took the box of tissues and the 'Tears of Joy' basket to the table with her and sat back down. I sat down and Char went back to the table to continue her toast.

"Trenice, you never gave up on me. I stopped believing in love until I met Jordan. I saw how happy he made you. Jordan if it wasn't for you encouraging me, I would've given up and missed out on the best thing to ever happen to me – Carl." Shaliyah didn't have to go far this time – she just picked up the box of tissues and handed it to Carl as he stood up.

"Thank God he kept you from giving up," Carl said as he grabbed Char into a kiss and the room erupted in applause.

"Get a room!" Tim yelled as the room erupted in laughter. Shaliyah made sure the tissues were placed in the 'Tears of Joy' basket and they both sat down.

"Jordan, you're the brother I needed when I needed you most," Jake said as he stood up. "We've been friends since I moved to Riverdale

Avenue before they built Phillips Towers. Since then, nobody has ever been able to come between us, and no one ever will be able to come between us – I love you man."

"I love you too," Jordan said as Jake left the table and Jordan stood up so they could hug each other. Shaliyah stood up to see if they needed tissues but it wasn't necessary. Jordan sat down and Jake went back to the table.

"Thank you for making Jordan so happy Trenice – he deserves it," Rachel said as she raised her glass.

Shaliyah didn't bother to get up when my mother stood up. My mother took a tissue from the box and said, "The biggest blessing in the world is to see your children happy. I know I have nothing to worry about," she said as she wiped her eyes, sipped her champagne, and sat down, and put her tissue in the 'Tears of Joy' basket.

Magic started playing, 'Mr. Goodbar,' by Alicia Myers as Grandma stood up. "Good job Jordan," She said as she sipped her champagne and sat down.

"Thank you," Jordan laughed.

"I couldn't have said it better myself," Miss April laughed as she stood up, already feeling a few glasses up champagne. "Well – actually I could – but I'ma let you have this one Gladys," she laughed as the room erupted in laughter and she sat back down.

"Jordan, you're everything I knew you would be," Miss June said as she stood up. "You've always been a good son, you've grown into a good man, and I know you'll be a great husband," she said as she sipped her champagne. Jordan stood up, ran to the table, and grabbed his mother into a hug.

"Thank you Mum Mum" he said with tears in his eyes.

"I'll be right back," Shaliyah yelled as she ran into the living room to grab another box of tissues, ran back to the table, and sat back down. Jordan and Miss June made sure to put their tissues in the 'Tears of Joy' basket before Shaliyah took the basket and the tissues around the room because we all needed tissues too – especially me.

When Shaliyah got back to the table Reverend Bruce stood up to speak. "God Bless you both," Reverend Bruce said.

"Amen!" Everyone said in unison.

"I can see you're off to a great start and you have a lot of support. I've been doing this for many years and I can always tell when it's really genuine," Reverend Bruce said with a smile as he sipped his champagne. "If you need me, I'm a phone call, walk, or ride away," he said as he started to put on his jacket. "I've got another wedding to prepare for and a sermon on Sunday, so I need to get going," he said as he headed towards the door.

"Good bye Reverend Bruce – thank you for everything," I said as Jordan and I stood up to hug him.

"I'll see myself out," he said as we went down the hall and out the door.

Magic started playing, 'And The Beat Goes On,' by the Whispers as the main course was being served. The servers placed Caesar Salad at all the tables. The cooking station had Chicken Francaise, Penne ala Vodka, Sausage & Peppers, Fried Calamari with Red Sauce, Sesame Chicken with Rice, and Eggplant Parmesan.

As Tish stood up to speak, it was obvious she had had one too many glasses of champagne but that didn't stop her from getting a refill before she picked up her glass to toast. She gulped down another glass of champagne and fell back down into her chair.

"Here's to the finer things in life – starting with our husband's" Monique said as she raised her glass.

"Thank you Baby," Khoury said as he pulled her into a kiss.

"Aww...," we all said in unison.

"Here's to paradise," Roberta laughed as she lifted her glass.

"Forever," James said as he pulled her into a kiss.

"Aww...," we all said in unison.

"Here's to fingerpaint," Diana said as she raised her glass.

"I love to fingerpaint!" Shaliyah yelled as the room erupted in laughter.

"So do I," Eric said as he looked at Diana mischievously.

"Here's to having plenty of room," Carolyn said as she raised her glass as 'Saturday Love' began to play.

"Here's to Saturday Love," Tim said as he raised his glass.

"Ready when you are," Harold said as he pulled Sherrie into a kiss.

"Aww…," we all said in unison.

"Here's to plenty of champagne!" Bunny said as she raised her glass.

"And crushed ice!" Scott laughed.

"You think you'll be thirsty later?" Bunny asked slyly.

"I'm always thirsty for you Baby," Scott said as he pulled her into a kiss.

"Aww…," we all said in unison.

Everyone got up from their seats when 'Got To Give It Up,' started playing. Jordan and I moved to the middle of the floor and danced as everyone danced around us, except for Char and Carl. "Honey – look," I whispered as I pointed them out. Char and Carl were slow dancing, gazing into each other's eyes, and kissing, totally oblivious to everyone else, totally enjoying each other.

"Trenice?" I looked around the room trying to figure out who was calling me. "Trenice!" Shaliyah yelled as she tugged on my dress.

"Yes Shaliyah – what is it?" I asked.

"Her name is Bunny – right?" she asked, pointing to my friend.

"Yes Shaliyah," I answered. I turned back to look at Carl and Char but they weren't there so I went back to dancing while Shaliyah ran up to my friend...

"Miss Bunny?"

"Yes Shaliyah?"

"Did you hop around a lot in your mom's tummy?"

"No I didn't," Bunny laughed.

"Why do they call you Bunny then?" Shaliyah.

"I was named after my father's favorite singer," Bunny answered.

"Ooohhh... you have the same name as a famous singer?" Shaliyah asked.

"Yes I do," Bunny answered. "Her name is Bunny DeBarge."

"Ohhhh woooww! Mommy! Guess What?" Shaliyah yelled as she ran to find my mother.

"Congratulations again – we gotta get going," Marlowe said as he came over to hug us.

"Damn – what time is it?" Jordan asked.

"Night time – and some of us have to work tomorrow," Chandler laughed as he hugged us.

"I love you Chandler," I laughed.

"I love you too Sis," he said.

"Welcome to the Family," Thelma said as she hugged us.

"Thank you," Jordan said.

"You know you stuck now right?" Sheila laughed as she hugged us.

"Yes I do," Jordan laughed.

"Good night y'all," Tina said as she hugged us.

"Good night Sis," Jordan said.

"I told y'all," Troy said as he hugged us.

"Yes you did," Smalls said as he hugged us, "But you didn't tell me nothin' I didn't already know," Smalls laughed.

"I'm so happy for y'all," Keisha said as she hugged us.

"Me too," Wayne said as he hugged us.

"What the hell took y'all so long?" Michelle laughed as she hugged us.

"Leave 'em alone Michelle," my mother laughed as she hugged us.

"Move Claire," Miss June said as she pushed her way through to hug us.

"Le'me git in there," Miss April laughed as she pushed her way through to hug us.

"Alright April," my grandmother laughed.

"I know it is!" Miss April laughed.

"You gonna move sometime today?" my grandmother laughed.

"Go on Gladys," Miss April laughed as she moved so my grandmother could come hug us.

"Don't forget where I live," Grandma said.

"Never," I whispered.

"Don't forget me!" Shaliyah yelled as she ran towards us and jumped into Jordan's arms.

"We could never do that Shaliyah," Jordan said as they hugged each other.

"Aww...," we all said in unison.

Jordan and I watched as they all left. Magic packed up his equipment as the servers cleaned up, and then they left. When we turned to our friends Jordan said, "I guess y'all are leaving soon too."

"Who said anything about leaving?" Rachel laughed.

Jordan and I looked at each other and smiled. We knew we were in for one hell of a night.

"Jordan, Trenice, - y'all sit here," Rachel instructed as she directed us to the living room. "They're ready!" she yelled as everyone else came into the living room and sat around us.

"The game is Truth or Dare – you tell the truth, you take the dare, or you get outta the game," Jake said.

"This is gonna be fun," Jordan said mischievously.

"I'll go first," Char said as she got up off the couch, knelt down in from of Carl, and took his hands in hers. "Carl – truth or dare?"

"Truth," Carl answered.

"Carl, I have never been as happy as I am when I'm with you. I love you with all my heart. Will you marry me?" she asked Carl as she pulled the engagement band she had from behind her back, opened the box, and placed the ring on his finger. We all sat quietly and anxiously waiting for his answer while he stared at the Black Diamond Wedding Band in 14K White Gold, with Treated Black Diamonds set in the center of the ring, engraved C & C. Carl's eyes swelled up with tears and he smiled through them as he bent down to take Char's face in his hands.

"Char, my love, my one and only, my forever, I didn't know what love was until you came into my life. I fell in love with you the moment I saw you, I've loved you ever since, and I want to keep on loving you for the rest of my life. Of course I'll marry you," he answered as he kissed her.

"Aww...," We all said in unison as went through all the tissues and filled up the 'Tears of Joy' basked with them.

"Welcome to the club," Jordan said as he pulled Carl into a hug.

"I'm so happy to be here," Carl said with tears in his eyes.

"Congratulations Brother," Jake said as he pulled Carl into a hug.

"Thank you Brother," Carl said.

"Congratulations," Paul said as he hugged Carl.

"Thank you," Carl said.

"Stop cryin'," Joe said as he pulled Carl into a hug with tears in his eyes too.

"I can't help it," Carl laughed.

"Monique proposed to me too," Khoury said as he pulled Carl into a hug.

"She did?" Carl asked.

"Yea – she got on one knee, opened the box with the ring in it, and said I'm yours if you'll have me," Khoury answered.

"What'd you say?" Carl asked.

"Shiiittt – I said the same thing you said – I told her of course I'll have you – you're the most beautiful woman in the world," Khoury answered.

"I love it when women propose," James said as he pulled Carl into a hug.

"So do I," Carl laughed. "I just never thought it would happen to me."

"Never say never," Eric said as he pulled Carl into a hug."

"You got that right," Carl said.

"You are blessed," Tim said as he pulled Carl into a hug.

"Amen!" Carl said.

"That's a good look," Harold said as he pulled Carl into a hug. "You keep messin' around you gonna wind up like me and Sherrie."

"Fine with me," Carl laughed.

"Le'me find out," Carlos laughed as he pulled Carl into a hug.

"Y'all engaged too?" Carl asked.

"I'm workin' on it," Carlos answered.

"Let's see who gets married first," Mike said as he pulled Carl into a hug.

"Y'all engaged too?" Carl asked.

"Yes we are," Mike answered.

"We'll get there one day," Scott said as he pulled Carl into a hug.

"Y'all not ready yet?" Carl asked.

"I'm not pushing it," Scott answered.

"What if she pushes you?" Carl asked.

"Then I'll fall down and pull her ass on top of me," Scott laughed.

"Girl, you did it!" I yelled as I grabbed her up off the floor and into a hug.

"He said yes – I can't believe it!" Char cried.

"Of course he said yes," Rachel said as she pulled Char into a hug. "He loves you Char."

"And I love him too," Char said.

"I'm so happy for you," Tish said as she pulled Char into a hug.

"Thank you Tish – I'm happy for you too," Char said.

"You're a lucky woman," Theresa said as she hugged Char.

"I know I am – I still can't believe he said yes," Char said.

"I knew he would say yes just like I knew Khoury would say yes," Monique said as she pulled Char into a hug.

"How'd you know?" Char asked.

"It's a gut feeling," Monique answered. "Just as you're sure you wanna ask them, you gotta be sure they'll say yes – otherwise, you wouldn't ask."

"James loves that shit," Roberta said as she hugged Char.

"He does?" Char asked.

"Yea – he thinks it's sexy when a woman is secure enough in herself to ask a man to marry her."

"So have you asked James to marry you?" Diana asked as she pulled Char into a hug.

"Not yet," Roberta answered.

"Girl, you're blessed!" Carolyn said as she pulled Char into a hug.

"Thank you Carolyn," Char said.

"I already see y'all gonna wind up like us," Sherrie laughed as she pulled Char into a hug.

"That's fine with me," Char laughed.

"God bless y'all," Diedre said as she pulled Char into a hug. "I guess me and Carlos will be the last one's to get married."

"Don't be so sure about that," Wanda said as she pulled Char into a hug.

"Y'all set a date yet?" Diedre asked.

"Why you rushin' me? You sound like Mike," Wanda laughed.

"Congratulations Char," Bunny said as she pulled Char into a hug.

"Thank you Bunny," Char said.

"Are you ever getting married Bunny?" Wanda asked.

"Never say never," Bunny laughed.

"This has been one hell of a wedding night," I laughed.

"Damn right – everybody's having fun - folks getting' engaged," Jordan laughed.

"Sorry y'all," Char said.

"I'm not," Carl laughed.

"Neither are we," Harold said as the room erupted in laughter.

"We've been here all night," Jake said.

"I guess we better get going," Rachel laughed.

"Good night y'all!" Carl yelled as he jumped up off the couch, pulled Char by the hand, and the two of them ran down the hallway and out the door.

"Well Damn!" Jake laughed.

"Let's go y'all," Rachel laughed.

"Good night y'all," I yawned.

"You mean good morning," Jordan yawned.

"Love y'all," somebody yelled as they let themselves out.

"Love y'all too," Jordan yawned on our way to the bedroom.

"Awww... Honey... look...," I said as I stopped by the guest room."

"Aww... that's nice," Jordan said as he peaked inside. The bed was made up with the

Red and Gold Trim Bed In A Bag and all our gifts were laid out on top of it.

"When did they have time to do all this?" I whispered.

"I have no idea – but I'm glad they did, because we have more important matters that need attending to... Mrs. Williams," he whispered in my ear as he pulled me close to him, picked me up, carried me into the master bedroom, laid me on the bed, unzipped my dress, slid it off of me, and placed it on the chair.

"Yes we do... Mr. Williams," I acknowledged as I watched Jordan undress, place his clothes in the chair, climb onto the bed, and pull me close to him.

"I love you Mrs. Williams," he said as he kissed me.

"I love you to Mr. Williams," I said as I kissed him back. "Did you put the password on the Wi-Fi?" I whispered.

"Yes Beautiful," Jordan whispered.

"Good because I have something to tell you," I yawned.

"What it is Beautiful?" Jordan whispered as he kissed my neck and began sliding his hand down my back, stopping to pull me closer...

"I'm pregnant," I answered. Jordan's eyes swelled up with tears.

"We're gonna have a baby?" he asked.

"Yes Honey... we're gonna have a baby," I answered.

"I love you sooo much Beautiful," he whispered.

"I love you too," I yawned.

"Good morning Beautiful," he said as he kissed me.

"Good morning Honey," I said as I kissed him back.

"Good morning Araura," he said as he got up, kissed my stomach, laid back beside me, and we both drifted off to sleep.

Chapter 105

"Good morning Beautiful," Jordan whispered as he nibbled on my ear."

"Good morning Honey," I whispered.

"Are you hungry?" he asked.

"Yeeeessss...,"

"Okay...," he said as he jumped up off the bed and headed towards the kitchen.

"I'll come keep you company," I said as I got up out the bed.

"Oh no you don't Mrs. Williams – you get back in that bed and stay there until I tell you to get up... if I tell you to get up," he laughed.

"Okay," I laughed as I got back into bed.

"Now that that's settled – what can I get you for breakfast?"

"Coffee..."

"Coffee coming up," he said. "What would you like to eat?"

"Scrambled eggs..."

"Would you like bacon or sausage?"

"I'd like sausage..."

"Would you like biscuits or pancakes?"

"Biscuits..."

"Cheese... in... the... eggs?"

"Yessss!"

"Okay then – I'll be back," he laughed as he jumped up off of me and darted out the bedroom towards the kitchen. I sighed, turned to my side, and watched Jordan dart down the hallway. "

"I'm so happy Araura," I whispered as I rubbed my stomach. "Your Daddy loves you, and so do I," I yawned as I drifted off back to sleep. My nap didn't last long (at least I felt like it didn't) because the smell of fresh coffee flavored with hazelnut creamer stirred my nostrils. I sat up in the bed, stretched, yawned, and looked for Jordan but he wasn't there. I turned to look at the coffee and watched the steam rising from it so I knew that Jordan was there while I was sleeping. "Might as well drink my coffee while it's hot," I said as I picked up my coffee to drink it, and noticed the nightstand drawer was slightly open. I bent over to close it and saw that Jordan took the pregnancy test out of the garbage and placed it in the nightstand. I smiled to myself as Jordan came into the bedroom and caught me closing the drawer.

"You're awake," he said as he smiled mischievously.

"Yes I am," I said as I picked up my coffee and started drinking it." When he came back into the bedroom he had a tray with two plates of scrambled eggs with cheese, sausage, and biscuits. Also on the tray were two small glasses of orange juice, and a bowl of fruit with kiwi, watermelon, cantaloupe, grapes, and strawberries. I sat upright in bed to take the tray from him so he could get in bed beside me. He took the two glasses of orange juice off the tray, set them on the night stand, climbed into bed beside, me, then started praying: "Lord, thank you for this food, that you for blessing us with Araura, and thank you for my beautiful wife," he prayed as he took my face in his hands and kissed me softly.

"Amen," I whispered as I kissed him back. Jordan took the tray off my lap, sat it in the middle of the bed, and we ate. "Damn, this is good," I said as I ate.

Chapter 106

When we woke up it was dark out. "What time is it?" I yawned.

"It's 8 o'clock," I said as we started kissing.

"Are you still hungry?" Jordan asked.

"The phone's ringing," I whispered.

"It's Vanessa," Jordan said as he sat up.

"Should we call her back?" I asked.

"Might as well," Jordan answered.

"Okay," I said as I dialed her number.

"Weichert Realty," she answered.

"Hi Vanessa," I yawned as I put the phone on speaker.

"Hi Trenice – how's everything?" Vanessa asked.

"Wonderful," Jordan answered.

"Glad to hear that – I'm sorry to disturb you but I have news," Vanessa said.

"Okay... What is it?" I asked.

"We have an offer on your condo," Vanessa answered.

"That sounds good," Jordan said.

"Well... the bad news is they can't come up to $450k," she said.

"Well what can they come up to?" I asked.

"They're only qualified for $250k – with a $100k down payment – and, they want you to pay the closing costs," Vanessa answered.

"They got some damn nerve," Jordan laughed.

"So I guess that's a no then?" Vanessa laughed.

"Not necessarily," I answered.

"What do you mean by that Trenice?" Vanessa asked.

"Well - $250k plus $100k is $350k – minus $13k in closing is $337k – minus $450k is a loss of $113k... hhmmm... that is a lot...," I said.

"Yes it is!" Jordan agreed.

"However, if we don't take this offer, we could continue paying $1,000 per month in maintenance for the next six months or so, which amounts to half of the closing costs anyway," I said.

"That's also true," Vanessa said.

"So what do you want to do Beautiful?"
Jordan asked.

"Vanessa, can you send us the offer so we
can take a look at it?" I asked.

"Sure I can Trenice – what would you like
me to tell them?"

"You can tell them we're considering it if
you want – but nothing definite," I answered.

"Okay Trenice – I wish it was a better
offer."

"Look at the bright side Vanessa –
properties in this building usually stay on the
market for months before they get an offer," I
said.

"That's because other realtors won't bother
giving the sellers anything but full price offers –
but I present my clients with all offers," Vanessa
said.

"Isn't that risky?" I asked. "What if the
listing expires before you get a full price offer?"

"What if y'all got the best realtor in the
region?" Vanessa boasted proudly.

"I know that's right!" Jordan laughed.

"Okay Trenice – I'll get this right over to
you," Vanessa said.

"Okay Vanessa – we'll get back to you," I
said.

"Talk to you soon," Vanessa said as she
hung up.

"Let me go in the kitchen and see what I
can find," Jordan said as he jumped up and

darted out the bedroom towards the kitchen. I got outta bed, snatched my lap top, got back into bed, and turned it on.

"Well Beautiful, it looks like we'll be eating dessert," Jordan yelled from the kitchen. I didn't answer him because I was too busy reading what Vanessa sent over. "Hey Beautiful —we don't have anything in there but cake," Jordan laughed as he came into the bedroom.

"Uh huh... that's nice...," I answered while continuing to go over the offer...

"What's wrong Trenice?" Jordan asked.

"Nothing Honey," I answered while continuing to read what was on the computer...

"Okay that's it – you haven't heard a word I said – what are you looking at?" he asked as he came to bed, snatched the laptop from me, and read: 'Buyer: Jake Earl Monroe.' "Oh... I see... this is interesting," he said as he continued reading the offer.

"It would be kinda nice to have them living downstairs," I said.

"Yes – it would be nice – but it wouldn't be nice," Jordan said.

"Why not?" I asked.

"I love my best friend – but he has a big family, and they're always visiting," he answered.

"That's nice," I said.

"Yes – it is nice – but they treat us like family too – so every time they visit him, they might visit us too," he laughed.

"So what's wrong with that?" I asked.

"Nothing – if you don't mind them dropping by unannounced," he laughed.

"Oh... I see...," I laughed.

"You can't just let it go to voice mail when they call – they'll come bang on the door talkin' 'bout you didn't answer the phone – I wanted to make sure you're okay," he laughed.

"Oh no!" I laughed.

"I don't see how Rachel lives with them – they never have any privacy," he laughed.

"Maybe that's why they want to move out," I said.

"Hmmm... I never thought of it that way... you might be right," he said.

"So what do you think of their offer," I asked.

"Well... I wish it was closer to asking... but I know they don't really have it," he answered.

"I know... but $113k is a lot to lose... you think they can pay the closing costs?" I asked.

"Maybe they can – but they're probably trying to have a cushion so they can have some money to furnish the condo – plus, I'm sure they wanna have some money in case something happens," Jordan answered.

"They won't have to worry about that in this building," I said.

"Jake wants to make sure he has money to take care of his mother," Jordan said. "He loves

Rachel to death but his mother is the most important woman in his life."

"Aww... That's sweet," I said.

"Not always," Jordan said.

"Why not?" I asked.

"Rachel and Jake's mom got into it a few times and Jake always sides with his mother," Jordan answered. "The last time they got into it, Jake and Rachel were arguing and she called him a motherfucker – mom got in the middle and told Rachel don't you call my son a motherfucker – you ain't never seen his shoes under my bed," Jordan laughed.

"That's crazy!" I laughed.

"Jake's mom is tough – Jake's lucky Rachel puts up with her," Jordan said. But I think his luck's about to run out."

"Why you say that?" I asked. "You think Rachel's gonna leave Jake?"

"Oh she'll never leave Jake – but she's not staying in his mother's house too much longer either," Jordan answered. "That's why they're looking for a place because he knows Rachel's ready to bounce and he doesn't want to lose her."

"So do you think we should accept their offer?" I asked.

"I'd consider it – but it's really up to you," Jordan answered.

"Let's do it!" I said.

"You sure Beautiful?" Jordan asked.

"There's 17 floors between us," I laughed.

"I hope we don't regret this," Jordan said.

"Why are you so worried Honey?" I asked.

"I don't want to ruin our friendship," Jordan answered.

"Didn't you live together growing up?" I asked.

"Yea, we did," Jordan answered.

"That wasn't too bad right?" I asked.

"It was great," Jordan answered with a smile.

"This will be great too," I said. "My best friend got engaged – her fiancée works downstairs – your best friend will live downstairs – who knows – maybe one day Char and Carl will buy a condo in this building too... "Hi Vanessa," I said as I quickly answered the phone.

"Hi Trenice," Vanessa said.

"We've decided to accept their offer!" I yelled as I put the phone on speaker.

"Hold on Trenice," Vanessa said.

"Is something wrong?" Jordan asked.

"Not at all," Vanessa answered.

"Okay... so what's up?" Jordan asked.

"I got you a better offer!" Vanessa yelled.

"You did?" I asked.

"Yes!" Vanessa answered.

"How much better?"Jordan asked.

"How 'bout full asking?" Vanessa answered.

"Wow!" I yelled.

"So do you accept?" Vanessa asked.

"Can we see it?" I asked.

"Why do you need to see it Trenice – never mind – I'll send it right over... bam!"

"Did she just hang up on you Beautiful?" Jordan asked.

"Yes she did," I sighed.

"That's fucked up," Jordan laughed.

"Yes it is," I said as I opened the offer.

"What's wrong Beautiful?" Jordan asked as I started to cry...

"Look...," I whispered.

"Jordan took the lap top, looked at it, read the offer, and dropped it on the bed. "Carl McIver," he whispered.

"What are we going to do?" I whispered.

"You're going to stop crying before we do anything," Jordan said as he pulled me close to him and wiped my tears. "It's not that serious," he said as he kissed my lips, then my eyes.

"How do we choose between two friends?" I asked as my eyes started tearing up again.

"Stop crying," Jordan said as he kissed me again and wiped my tears.

"Honey – you don't understand – she's been through so much," I whispered.

"I know Beautiful – I was there – remember?" he laughed.

"Yes, I remember," I laughed.

"I think you should take the full price offer," Jordan said.

"I wish there was another condo going up for sale so we didn't have to choose," I whispered.

I know how much you love Char," Jordan said.

"And I know how much you love Jake and Rachel – and I love them too," I said.

"Listen to me Beautiful," Jordan said as he picked up my chin to look me in my eyes. "Yes – I love my best friend – but business is business, and if my best friend loves me, he wouldn't want us to lose $113k," Jordan said as he kissed me.

"You won't be mad?" I whispered.

"If the situation were reversed – and they offered full asking instead of Char and Carl – what would you want me to do?" Jordan asked.

"I would want you to take the full price offer – especially because it's your best friend," I said sadly.

"They'll find something else Beautiful," Jordan said.

"I don't want them to be mad at us," I whispered.

"What if they both offered the same price? What would you do then?" Jordan asked.

"I don't know what I'd do," I sighed.

"Do you trust me?" Jordan asked.

"Of course," I answered.

"Then trust me when I tell you they'll be just fine," Jordan said.

"Okay," I answered.

"Now call Vanessa so we can get back to business," Jordan said as he started kissing me on my neck...

"Weichert – Hi Trenice," Vanessa said as she answered the phone.

"You aiight?" Jordan laughed.

"I'm sorry about that – I spilled my coffee and I needed to get it up before it got to my computer," she said.

"It sounded like you were mad because Trenice wanted to see the full price offer," Jordan laughed.

"Not at all," Vanessa said. "I was taken aback though," she laughed.

"The first offer was from our friends you met at the wedding," I said.

"Oh... I see," Vanessa said.

"The full price offer is from one of the best men at our wedding," Jordan said.

"Ooohhh... I had no idea," Vanessa said." So what are you going to do?"

"We're going with the full price offer," I answered.

"That's wonderful! You can close in two weeks," Vanessa said.

"We can?" I asked.

"You didn't read the offer did you Trenice?" Vanessa asked.

"No I didn't," I answered.

"He's paying cash," Vanessa said.

"Oh my God!" I yelled.

"Carl's ballin' like that?" Jordan asked.

"Carl's ballin' like that," Vanessa laughed.

"Char's gonna be so happy," I said.

"What's Char got to do with this?" Vanessa asked.

"Char proposed to Carl last night and he said yes," Jordan answered.

"Wait a minute... are you telling me that the man who's buying your condo is her fiancé?" Vanessa asked.

"Yes Vanessa," I answered.

"So she proposed to him last night?"

"Yea," Jordan answered.

"And now he's buying her a home," Vanessa sighed. "You're right Trenice – Char's going to be really happy. Le'me go so I can make this happen – I'll see you soon."

"Bye Vanessa," Jordan and I said in unison as she hung up.

"Who's banging on the door?" I mumbled.

"I'll be right back – don't move Beautiful," Jordan said as he grabbed his robe, threw it on, and I caught a glimpse of his ass peeking out before he closed it to go down the hall to answer the door...

"Hey Jordan – how are ya?" I recognized Sami Sosa's voice from Sam's Pizzeria and smiled.

"I'm good – and hungry," Jordan laughed.

"Where's Trenice?" he asked.

"She's relaxing," Jordan answered.

"Tell her I said hello," he said as he handed Jordan the bag.

"I will Sami – see ya later," Jordan said as he closed the door. When he came back into the bedroom I bust out laughing. "I had to do it – I'd still be standing there if I didn't," Jordan said as he handed me a plate of spaghetti with chicken broccoli, garlic, and oil.

"Thank you Honey," I said.

"And here I go," Jordan said as he sat next to me with a plate of chicken parmigiana and spaghetti.

"That looks good," I said.

"Lord, bless this food, and thank you for blessing us – amen," Jordan said.

"Amen – can I have some?" I laughed.

"Here Beautiful," Jordan said as he fed me a piece of chicken parmigiana.

"I love you Honey," I said as I started eating my food.

"I love you too Beautiful," Jordan said as we ate.

Chapter 107

"What time is it?" I yawned as I heard the phone ring.

"It's too damn early – that's what time it is," Jordan answered as he rolled over to look at the phone. "It's Tyler – might as well get it," he said as he answered the phone. "Good morning Tyler! What can you do for me today?" he laughed as he put the phone on speaker...

"I can accompany you down to the precinct so these detectives can stop aggravating me," Tyler answered.

"They still bothering you? What the fuck do they want anyway? A confession? Fine – I'll tell them I did it!" Jordan laughed.

"Please tell me you're joking," Tyler sighed.

"Of course I'm joking Tyler – what's wrong?" Jordan asked.

"Nothing – I'm just having a bad morning – I'm handling a divorce and no matter what I do for my client, the bitch just won't fuckin' let up – he should've never married her in the first got damned place – oh my God – I'm soooo sorry – that was completely unprofessional of me – how y'all doin?"

"We're great Tyler," I yelled.

"I'm glad to hear somebody's happy," Tyler said. "Clients like you make everything I go through worth it."

"Awww... thank you Tyler," I said.

"See – that's what I'm talkin' about – I can see your smile from here," Tyler said.

"When do you need me Tyler?" Jordan asked.

"Well... they want to see you down at the precinct as close to 9 a.m. as possible..."

"They'll see me by 12:00 today," Jordan said.

"Can't you do it earlier Jordan? Please?"

"Tyler, its Sunday!" Jordan exclaimed.

"I know – but they change shifts early and – you know what – that's not your problem – I'll call them and..."

"I'll come earlier Tyler," Jordan interrupted.

"You sure Jordan?" Tyler asked.

"I'm as sure as you're buying coffee," Jordan laughed.

"You got it – what time can you be there?" Tyler asked.

"We can be there by 10:00 Tyler," I answered.

"They only want to see Jordan Trenice," Tyler said.

"I can wait in the waiting area," I said.

"Alrighty then – see you at the precinct at 10:00," Tyler said as he hung up. When we got downstairs to the lobby Carl was all smiles. "Good morning Mr. & Mrs. Williams, he beamed. "I need to talk to y'all about…"

"We gotta go Carl – we'll talk when we get back," Jordan said as he grabbed my hand, pulled me through the lobby door, and we headed down North Broadway to the precinct.

Chapter 108

When we got to the precinct, Tyler was sitting there with three cups of coffee. "I thought you said you'd be here by 10 a.m.," Tyler laughed.

"What time is it?" Jordan laughed.

"10:15," Tyler laughed.

"Sorry about that man," Jordan said.

"No need to apologize," Tyler laughed. "You're actually early – Detective Rosa won't be here until 10:30," he laughed again. "I actually thought this coffee was gonna get cold," he said as he handed me a cup, and then Jordan.

"Thanks man – you're the best," Jordan said.

"Can I get you to put that in writing?" Tyler asked.

"Absolutely," Jordan said.

"Good morning Mr. Marshall, Mr. Williams, I'm Detective Morack - Detective Rosa is here so we'll be starting shortly – this way please..."

"Good morning Detective," I said sarcastically.

"This way please," he repeated.

"Don't be rude to my wife," Jordan snapped.

"Excuse me?" Detective Morack asked.

"My wife spoke to you," Jordan said.

"I wasn't speaking to her!" he snapped.

"You know what mothafucka?" Jordan asked as he stepped towards him. Tyler pushed Jordan back as Detective Barros came out into the lobby.

"Do we have a problem here?" he asked, looking Jordan directly in the eyes.

"Yea we got a fuckin' problem – my wife said good morning and Detective Morack told me he wasn't speaking' to her!" Jordan snapped. Detective Rosa walked into the lobby.

"Detective Rosa – please take Mr. Williams and his attorney into the first door on the left – Mrs. Williams, I apologize for his behavior – Detective Morack – come with me," Detective Barros said as Detective Morack followed him into the office and slammed the door...

"I'm sick of your shit!" Detective Morack yelled.

"If you're so sick of my shit – put in your fuckin' papers – it isn't my fault or anyone else's that your wife left you – you may have gotten away with that shit in the other precinct but you're not getting away with it here – I have enough complaints in your file to put you on administrative leave – and trust me – you won't get paid – and you won't have to worry about your wife taking your house because you won't have one left for her to take – and if you think I'm playing with you – try me!" Detective Barros yelled. I was stunned. Detective Morack walked out of Detective Barros's office and down the hall right past me and went into the room on the left where Jordan and Tyler were. I didn't have to listen too hard because no one was whispering…

"Is everything okay Mrs. Williams?" Detective Barros asked.

"Yes, I'm okay," I answered.

"Can I get your more coffee?" he asked.

"No thank you – I'm good," I answered.

"Okay then – if you change your mind, just come get me," he said as he went back into his office…

"Thank God," I said out loud as I turned my attention towards the room on the left…

"So when was the last time you saw Dr. Aiden?" Detective Morack asked.

"I don't remember," Jordan answered.

"You're full of shit!" Detective Morack snapped.

"Detective Morack, that isn't necessary," Tyler said.

"He's right," Detective Rosa said.

"Actually, I'm not full of shit – I haven't had breakfast yet," Jordan laughed, "but let me know where the bathroom is in case I need to use it," he laughed again.

"Mr. Williams, this isn't funny," Detective Rosa said.

"The hell it ain't," Jordan said. Tyler put his hand on Jordan's shoulder. "I'm good Tyler," he said, "but this shit here is hilarious – this is worse than an old episode of law and order," he laughed.

"I've had just about enough of you!" Detective Morack yelled.

"Oh so you Robo Cop now?" Jordan laughed. "I could'a wrote a better script then this," he laughed again.

"Mr. Williams – please excuse my partner – something's wrong with him." Detective Rosa said.

"Tell me something I don't know," Jordan laughed.

"You don't know we have video surveillance of you running through the parking lot right before we found Dr. Aiden dead in his car," Detective Rosa said.

"Is that right?" Jordan asked.

"Yes – that's right," Detective Rosa answered.

"Okay...," Jordan said.

"So do you have an explanation for what you were doing in the parking lot?" Detective Rosa asked.

"No I don't – and I don't need one," Jordan answered.

"Yes you do," Detective Rosa said and Detective Morack smirked.

"Why's that?" Jordan asked.

"Because you're a suspect," Detective Rosa answered.

"Because I ran through a parking lot? Get the fuck outta here!" Jordan laughed.

"Because you ran through the parking lot shortly before Dr. Aiden was killed," Detective Morack said.

"You sure about that?" Jordan asked.

"Unfortunately for you... yes," Detective Morack answered. "It's not like anyone would blame you if you did it – after all – we saw what he did to your wife," Detective Morack sneered.

"Lord please...," I started praying, but God was right on it, answering the prayer I started as Jordan spoke...

"Let me tell you something Detective Morack," Jordan said as he stood up. I could see his silhouette through the glass. Tyler tried to pull Jordan back to sit down but Jordan wasn't having it... "If I killed Dr. Aiden – I've worked at

that hospital since before you got to this precinct
– I know where every camera is – I wouldn't be
stupid enough to kill him in the parking lot
where I could be seen, and then leave him in his
car," Jordan said as he continued to stand.

"I never said you were stupid," Detective
Morack sneered.

"You never said you had any evidence
either," Jordan said.

"Mr. Williams – you had motive, you had
means, and you had opportunity," Detective Rosa
said.

"If you were sure about that you'd be
placing me under arrest," Jordan said.

"We can arrest you anytime we want,"
Detective Morack said.

"Tyler, my coffee's wearing off and we
haven't had breakfast - I'm ready to go," Jordan
said as he got up and started towards the door...

"Mr. Williams we're not done," Detective
Rosa said.

"You may not be done, but I am – have a
nice day gentlemen," Jordan said as he opened
the door and saw me standing there. "You comin'
Tyler?" Jordan asked as he put his arm around
my waist and pulled me close to him.

"I guess I am," Tyler laughed. "Where are
we going?"

"Parkside Diner," Jordan and I said in
unison.

"Okay," Tyler laughed. "Oh shoot – that's my phone – I need to take this – I'll meet you outside," Tyler said as he ran out the front door.

"Jordan?" I asked.

"Yes Beautiful?" he answered.

"Never mind," I said.

"Everything okay Mr. Williams?" Detective Barros asked.

"Yes sir!" Jordan answered as he pulled me closer to him.

"Glad to hear it – have a good day," he said as we walked towards the front door.

"Wait a minute Honey," I said as I turned to throw my empty coffee cup away... and watched Detective Rosa hand Detective Barros a tape...

When we got to Parkside Diner we were seated right away. As soon as we got comfortable, I told Tyler and Jordan what I saw. "I saw Detective Rosa pass a tape to Detective Barros."

"When?" Jordan asked.

"When I went to throw my cup away," I answered.

"Muthafuckas!" Jordan exclaimed.

"Don't worry about it," Tyler said.

"Why shouldn't I worry about it?" Jordan asked.

"Because it's procedure," Tyler answered.

"I thought they only did that when you got arrested?" I asked.

"They do that with everyone," Tyler answered.

"Why?" Jordan asked.

"Because of dicks like Detective Morack," Tyler answered. "He wasn't supposed to treat you like that in the interrogating room."

"He wasn't?" Jordan asked.

"Hell no! He went way over the line – especially when he told you he saw what Dr. Aiden did to your wife."

"I caught that," Jordan said.

"I started praying," I said.

"Oh you heard that Trenice?" Tyler asked.

"I heard everything Tyler," I answered.

"Damn – I'm glad I'm on your side – you're dangerous," Tyler laughed. I didn't laugh with him because I didn't think it was funny – true – but not funny. Jordan caught the look on my face and continued.

"Tyler, I'm good at bait," Jordan said.

"What do you mean?" Tyler asked.

"You watch enough episodes of Law & Order, you figure it out," Jordan laughed.

"What did you figure out?" Tyler asked.

"There's a reason you always get questioned at the precinct," Jordan answered. "If they have something on you already, they arrest you. If they don't have anything on you, they try and bait you so you'll flip out or you'll slip up – this way then can arrest you and detain you for 24 hours – this gives them more time to dig."

"Damn – you're even more dangerous than you're wife," Tyler laughed. Jordan didn't crack a smile.

"Here's your coffee," the waitress said when she placed two cups of coffee on our table.

"Would you like coffee as well sir?" she asked Tyler.

"No thank you," Tyler answered.

"Okay – that'll be one short stack with bacon and two eggs medium – don't break the yolk – with corned beef hash and white toast – light with butter – what can I get you sir?"

"I'll have scrambled with sausage," Tyler answered.

"Will that be white, wheat, or rye?" she asked.

"Rye," Tyler answered.

"With home fries or grits, or French fries?" she asked.

"Home fries," Tyler answered.

"I'll be back shortly," she said.

"I'm impressed," Tyler said.

"Yea – we're regulars here," Jordan said.

"I like the waitress," Tyler said.

"So do we," I said.

"Well I'm sure glad that's over," Tyler said.

"Me too," Jordan said as the waitress brought our food to the table.

"Can I get you anything else?" she asked.

"No thanks," I said.

"Enjoy your breakfast – and thank you for choosing Parkside," she said as she went to another table.

"I have to admit – I was worried," Tyler said.

"I wasn't worried at all," Jordan said.

"I could tell," Tyler laughed.

"I didn't do anything to be worried about – at least nothing they know if," Jordan laughed.

"Umm… should I be hearing this?" Tyler asked.

"No you shouldn't – you should be hearing the fork hit your plate 'cause this food is slammin'!" Jordan said as we ate.

Chapter 109

"Are you sure you want to go to work today?" Jordan asked as he spooned me.

"I'm not going to work Honey – I'm just dropping these papers off to Personnel," I said as I snuggled next to him.

"Can't you drop them off on another day?" he asked as I tried to get out of bed and he pulled me back in...

"Yes... I... could...," I answered between kisses...," but then I'd have to wait for the name change."

"You already changed your name," he said as he continued kissing me...

"Yes I did... but I want to go back to work as Mrs. Williams," I said.

"Okay then," he said as he got up. I'll go see Jake while you go drop off those papers, then we'll meet up later Beautiful," he said as he kissed me outta bed.

"Okay then – sounds good to me – besides – I'm not trying to spend all day there anyway," I laughed.

"You better not," he laughed as he got in the shower. I turned on News 12 and listened to Jeanine Rose state the following:

"We interrupt our regularly scheduled program to bring you this update. Police are still investigating Dr. Aiden's death. Although they have a suspect, no arrests have been made. We now return to our regularly scheduled programming."

"And there won't be any arrests made either," Jordan whispered. "What's wrong Beautiful? You look like you've seen a ghost... are you okay?" he asked me as he started getting dressed.

"I'm okay – you just scared the shit outta me," I laughed nervously.

"That's what you get for not joining me in the shower," he laughed.

"If I joined you in the shower... we'd still be in there," I said.

"What's wrong with that?" he asked.

"Nothing," I answered as I got in the shower. I turned on the water, got the loofah, got the body wash, and kept replaying what I had just seen and heard on News 12 as I washed... "Could he?" I asked myself. "Hell yea!" I answered. "I wonder if he did it though. Well if he did... thank you Lord," I said as I got out the shower and came into the bedroom.

"Who are you talkin' to Beautiful?" Jordan asked.

"I was talkin' to God," I answered as I got dressed.

"Okay... you ready," he asked.

"Yes I am," I smiled.

"Let's do this then," he said as we grabbed his wallet, my pocketbook, our keys, and we headed out. "Call me when you're done so I can meet you," he said, then kissed me good bye.

"I will Honey," I said. 'I love you."

"I love you too Beautiful – see you later," he said as he headed down North Broadway, and I headed towards White Plains. As I started to cross the street I saw an unmarked black Lincoln town car out the corner of my eye.

"Hmmm... I wonder what they're doing here... oh well – here comes the bus," I said to myself as I got on. I sat towards the back where the windows were bigger so I could admire the view. The ride was long but it was such a beautiful sight to see the children swimming in the pool as you went through Hastings, the mansions in Dobbs Ferry, the golf courses in Greenburg, and the mini mall on Tarrytown Road as you got near Downtown White Plains. I saw so many people hustling to get off the bus to make their connecting buses and trains, and I thanked God I wasn't one of them. When we pulled up in front of Macy's, I decided I wanted to treat myself to a Grande Carmel Machiatta so I went inside Starbucks and stood in line. The line was long but since I wasn't in a hurry to get to work, I enjoyed the smells of coffee, cookies, and sandwiches before I was interrupted...

"Miss? What can I get you?" the cashier asked.

"Oh – sorry – I'll have a Grande Carmel Machiatto – light and sweet." I answered.

"Name please?" the cashier asked.

"Trenice," I answered as I turned to look out the window and saw another unmarked black Lincoln town car.

"That'll be $5.04," the cashier said, interrupting me again.

"Here you go," I said as I handed her a $10 bill.

"I wish you'd pay attention – I haven't got all day – some of us have to get to work!" the man standing behind me snapped.

"Aww... Am I moving to slow for you?" I asked sarcastically as the cashier handed me a $5 bill. "Thanks – but I owe you 4 cents," I said deliberately.

"That's okay – I already closed the register," the cashier said, then turned to the man in back of me and said, "May I help you?"

"Yes you could – if she would MOVE!" he yelled in my ear.

"I need to see your manager," I told the cashier.

"Did I offend you in some way?" the cashier asked.

"Please get me your manager," I repeated. I smiled to myself as the man behind me was huffing and sucking his teeth...

"Is there a problem Maam?" the manager asked.

"Yes there is," I answered. This cashier was being very courteous – my total came to $5.04 – but because he started getting agitated and demanded I 'MOVE' out his way, she gave me back $5 instead of $4.96 – and now she can't open the drawer so I can give her 4 cents," I said.

"Is that right?" the manager asked.

"Damn right its right – she's in my way and I need to get to work!" he yelled.

"The customer is always right – let me help you with that," the manager said as he came from behind the counter, took him by the arm, and escorted him out the door.

"You know what – fuck that bitch and fuck you too!" he yelled as he stormed off.

"Don't worry about the 4 cents – here's your coffee – you have a nice day," the manager said as he handed me my coffee.

"Thank you – I sure will," I laughed. "That'll teach that muthafucka to fuck wit me – if Jordan was here he would'a punched him in his fuckin' face!" I laughed as I started walking down Court Street and noticed that same unmarked black Lincoln town car following me. "Why is this car following me? I know damn well I didn't steal this coffee – I must be buggin' – le'me get where I'm going," I said as I continued walking down Court Street until I got to East Post Road. I made a right and started walking towards 112 East Post Road and saw that same unmarked black Lincoln town car following me as I look to the left. "This some bullshit," I said. I slowed down and stopped in front of the gift shop pretending to look at something in the window and watched as the unmarked black Lincoln town car pulled up past me and parked in front of the building. "Oh they got jokes – okay – let's play," I said as I walked to the entrance and into the building.

"Good morning," Detective Barros said as I walked through the turnstile.

"Good morning!" I exclaimed. "You're working here now?"

"Just for today," he answered. "You work here?" The first thing that came to my mind was you know got damned well I work here – but I felt God's hand on my shoulder easing my temper...

"Yes I do – see this hallway?" I pointed out as I walked up behind the desk and showed him the hallway monitored by the camera.

"Oh – that's your area?" he asked.

"Yes – we're under constant surveillance – for our protection and theirs," I laughed.

"Have a nice day," I said as I got in the elevator. When I got off on the 5th floor Ms. Tyree stopped to look me up and down.

"Shall I strike a pose for you?" I laughed as I posed.

"Girl, you crazy," she laughed. "At least you didn't break anything this time," she laughed as she went down the hall.

"Welcome back – congratulations," Ms. Raynor said as she met me in reception.

"Thank you – here's everything," I said as I handed her the envelope.

"Thank you Trenice – make sure you stop at CSEA before you leave – I'll see you when you get back," she said as she got up and went back to her office. I got back in the elevator and ran right into Junio.

"Ola Chica – congratulations," he said as he kissed me on the cheek. "You comin' to see me?"

"Of course," I laughed. We walked down the hall together into the union office and I handed Fran my papers.

"Congratulations sweetie – we'll take care of this right away – don't forget to tell the credit union," she said.

"I won't – have a nice day," I said as I left. "Hmm... I might as well stop and say hi," I said as I got off on my floor and went down the hall. When I let myself in, Vilma was all smiles.

"Hey! Congratulations!" she said as she hugged me.

"Thank you," I said. "Where is everybody?"

"Hearings – where else?" she laughed.

"Oh God – that could take all morning – and I gotta go – I'll see you in two weeks," I said as I started back down the hallway...

"Good morning Trenice – may we speak with you?" Detective Morack asked.

"Why?" I answered.

"Calm down – we just have a few questions," Detective Rosa said.

"In order for me to calm down I'd have to be upset – which I'm not – let me see if there's a hearing room available – I don't need everybody in my business," I said as I took out my cell phone, hit video, then record before I went into the hearing room, sat down, and closed the door...

"Let's get to it – we know your husband killed Dr. Aiden – and he's not going to get away with it," Detective Morack snapped.

"If you have something to discuss regarding Dr. Aiden's murder – you can speak with my attorney – we're done here," I said as I got up from the table and attempted to leave...

"Sit your ass down!" Detective Rosa said as he stood in front of me.

"The hell you say!" I said as I pushed past him to grab the door knob...

"I don't give a damn what Dr. Aiden did to you," Detective Morack said as he came up behind me, pulled me back towards the table, and threw me in the chair. "You're not going anywhere," he whispered. I felt God's hand on my shoulder again – but this time he wasn't calming my anger – and Detective Morack was about to feel the rath of God through me...

"Don't you ever put your fuckin' hands on me again!" I screamed as I jumped up outta the chair, lunged across the table, and slammed my cell phone into his head, busting it open. Detective Rosa stepped to the side as Detective Morack wiped the blood from his head, stood up, and took out his handcuffs.

"Thank you for assaulting me – now I can place you under arrest," he said as he cuffed me.

"I'll take this," Detective Rosa said as he took my phone.

"Oh no you won't – I'll take that," Detective Barros said as he slammed the door open, came into the hearing room, and snatched the phone from him.

"Ricky – we can explain..." Detective Rosa tried to speak but Detective Barros cut him off...

"Take those cuffs off of her – now!" he yelled. Detective Morack started towards me and I backed away from him with my hands still cuffed behind my back towards Detective Barros... "Never mind – I'll do it," he said as he removed the cuffs... "Rosa – you get your ass back to the precinct – Morack – you get your ass downstairs and wait for the Chief – you're fuckin' done!"

"She assaulted me – she should be under arrest!" Detective Morack yelled.

"Shut the fuck up and take your ass downstairs like I told you to before I assault you!" Detective Barros yelled. "Here Trenice," he said as he tried to give me my cell phone.

"Keep it," I said.

"Why do I need to keep your phone?" he asked.

"I'll show you," I said as I took the phone and played the video for him.

"You don't need to give me your phone – I can take the video and transfer it to my phone," he said as he took out his phone, transferred the video to my phone, and handed my phone back to me. "I'll take you down to the precinct so you can file a complaint – are you hurt?" he asked.

"My back hurts," I answered.

"Do you need to go to the hospital?" he asked.

"I don't think so," I answered.

"We're going to the hospital," he said.

"Okay," I sighed. We got to the hospital in about 5 minutes. I thought we we're going straight to the waiting area but we went straight to the back instead.

"I need you to take care of her right away," Detective Barros said to the nurse.

"Doctor – we have a patient in custody that needs to be seen right away," the nurse said.

"I'm not in custody," I said.

"Excuse me?" the nurse snapped.

"She's not in custody," Detective Barros said.

"Well she can wait in the waiting room like everyone else then!" the nurse snapped.

"Do I need to repeat myself?" Detective Barros asked. "Do you know what protocol is? Do I need to have a reprimand put in your personnel file to remind you?"

"No sir – let me get the doctor for you," she said as she hurried around the corner. When she came back with the doctor he was all smiles.

"Ricky! How are ya?"

"Not to good," Detective Barros answered.

"What's wrong Ricky? It is your back again?" the doctor asked.

"Long story – I need her seen right away," Detective Barros answered, pointing towards me.

"What seems to be the problem dear," the doctor asked.

"I hurt my back," I answered.

"How did you hurt your back?" the doctor asked.

"He threw me into the chair," I mumbled.

"Who did that? Your husband? Is that why you're here Ricky? Is she pressing charges?"

"Yes she is – but it wasn't her husband – it was Detective Morack," Detective Barros said.

"How the hell does he keep getting away with this?" the doctor asked as he started massaging my back...

"I wasn't there before – but I was there today!" Detective Barros snapped.

"Nurse – get her down to x-ray right away – in the meantime, I'll get started on your paperwork," the doctor said.

"I can't take any x-rays," I said.

"Why not? How are we supposed to see what's going on with your back?" the nurse snapped.

"I'm pregnant," I answered.

"You're pregnant?" the nurse asked, softening her tone.

"You're pregnant?" Detective Barros asked.

"Who's pregnant?" the doctor asked as he came back with the paperwork.

"I'm pregnant," I answered.

"Who's your doctor?" the doctor asked.

"Dr. Campana," I answered.

"Nurse – get her down to ultra sound ASAP," the doctor said. "I'll get Dr. Campana on the phone," he said as he walked down the hall.

"I'll be back," Detective Barros said.

"Come with me Trenice," the nurse said as she took me by the hand. "Don't you worry – I'm sure your baby's just fine," she said as we got on the elevator. When we got off the elevator Dr. Campana was waiting for me.

"Hey Tyler," Jordan said as he answered his phone.

"Meet me at White Plains Hospital," Tyler said.

"Why do I need to meet you at White Plains Hospital?" Jordan asked.

"It's Trenice," Tyler answered.

"Trenice? What the fuck is going on Tyler?" Jordan snapped.

"I'll explain everything when I see you – but for now I need you to meet me at White Plains Hospital," Tyler repeated.

"I'm on my way," Jordan said as he hung up.

"What's wrong?" Jake asked.

"I need you to take me to White Plains Hospital," Jordan answered.

"What happened?" Jake asked.

"Tyler wouldn't tell me," Jordan answered. "I swear to God... if they hurt my wife or my child..."

"Your child? Trenice is pregnant?" Jake asked.

"Yea," Jordan answered.

"Le'me get you to the hospital," Jake said as they got in the car.

"Do they know what happened to Dr. Aiden?" Jake asked.

"They don't have a fuckin' clue," Jordan laughed. "They claim I'm a suspect because they saw me in the parking lot right before he died," Jordan laughed again.

"How do they know you were in the parking lot?" Jake asked.

"They have me on surveillance," Jordan answered.

"Damn man! What did you say?" Jake asked.

"I told them exactly what they wanted to hear," Jordan laughed.

"And what was that?" Jake asked.

"The truth!" Jordan laughed.

"What? Are you crazy?" Jake yelled... "Never mind – what exactly did you say to them?"

"I told them yes I was in the parking lot before he died, no I don't remember what I was doing there, and I didn't have to give them an explanation," Jordan laughed.

"You sure that was a good idea?" Jake asked.

"Trust me... you taught me well," Jordan said reassuringly. As soon as they got to the hospital Jordan went right in when he saw Tyler...

"Where is my wife?" Jordan asked.

"Jordan – I know you're upset – but I need you to stay calm," Tyler answered.

"And I really need you to tell me where my wife is," Jordan repeated. Tyler had never seen this look on Jordan's face. Jordan knew Tyler was afraid of what he might do.

"Are you okay Jordan?" Tyler asked.

"Is my wife okay?" Jordan asked.

"Are you Mr. Williams?" the nurse asked as she came out the double doors into the lobby.

"Yes I am," Jordan answered.

"Come with me," she said. Jordan followed her through the double doors.

"C'mere Trenice," Dr. Campana said as she pulled me into a hug and walked me into the examination room. "As soon as you get undressed, put this gown on and I'll be right back," she said.

"Can you stay?" I asked.

"Sure," she answered and sat in the chair. "Did you get married yet?" she asked as I got undressed and put on the gown.

"We got married on Friday," I answered.

"Oh my God! Congratulations! Where's your husband?"

"He's not here," I answered with tears in my eyes.

"Oh my God... what happened?" she asked as I got up on the table.

"I didn't want you to find out I was pregnant like this," I whispered. "We found out I was pregnant last week. We were waiting until my next appointment..."

"Why are you here Trenice?" Dr. Campana snapped.

"Are you mad at me?" I asked.

"Hell no – but when I'm on call and my favorite patient winds up in the emergency room – without her husband – I know it isn't good," she snapped as she put the gel on me. "Let's see how your baby is doing," she said as she started the ultra sound. "Oh my God," she whispered.

"What's wrong?" I whispered.

"You have a beautiful little baby in here," she beamed. "You have no scar tissue – the uterus looks good – sit up and take a look," she said as she raised the bed so I could see.

"Hi Araura," I said.

"Dr. Campana?" the nurse called outside the door.

"Yes nurse?" Dr. Campana answered.

"Her husband's here," she said as Jordan opened the door.

"Hi Araura," Jordan said as he took my hand, kissed my forehead, and continued to look at our baby on the screen.

"Would you like a picture?" she asked.

"Yea," we both answered in unison.

"Have you experienced any spotting or cramping?"

"No I haven't," I answered. "I told Detective Barros my back was hurting – next thing you know – I'm here," I answered.

"Your back just started hurting? You didn't fall or pull it at work lifting boxes?"

"I wasn't at work today," I answered. "I went to drop off some papers, I ran into Detective Barros, I told him my back was hurting, and here I am."

"Either he thinks you're really special – which I'm sure he does – or you're not telling me everything – but the most important thing is that you and Jordan are going to have a healthy baby," Dr. Campana said. "Dr. Campana?" the nurse called outside the door.

"Yes nurse?" Dr. Campana answered.

"I don't mean to rush you – but we have an emergency..."

"I'm on my way – congratulations you two – call me in a few weeks," she said as she opened the door and flew down the hall.

"Let's get you dressed so we can get outta here," Jordan said as he closed the door. I dressed quickly and we headed down the hall. "Thank you Lord," he said as we got in the elevator.

"Amen," I agreed. As soon as we got off the elevator, we ran into Detective Barros.

"Are you ready to go?" he asked.

"Yes we are," Jordan answered.

"We're almost done," Detective Barros said.

"I thought we could leave the hospital," Jordan said.

"You can leave the hospital – but I need Trenice to come down to the precinct," Detective Barros said.

"Is everything okay Trenice?" the doctor asked before Jordan got a chance to ask any questions...

"Yes – my baby's fine," I beamed.

"Thank God," he said. "You can leave with Detective Barros – have a nice day," he said as he picked up another chart to go check on the next patient.

"Hey!" Jake said as he picked me up in a bear hug.

"Hi Jake," I laughed as he put me down. "Hi Tyler."

"You okay Trenice?" Tyler asked.

"Yea," I answered.

"Are you ready?" Detective Barros asked.

"Yes I'm ready," I answered.

"Ready for what?" Jake asked.

"Who are you?" Detective Barros asked.

"This is my brother-in-law, Jake," I answered. "This is Detective Barros," I said as I introduced them.

"Nice meeting you – who's riding with us?" he asked.

"I'm riding with Trenice," Jordan answered.

"And you're both riding with me," Jake said.

"I guess I'll follow you," Tyler said.

"Okay then – let's go," Detective Barros said. When we got to the precinct, Detective Barros didn't waste any time.

"Let's go Trenice," he said as I followed him inside the precinct.

"You comin' Jake?" Jordan asked.

"Naa... I'll wait in the car until you're done," he answered.

"C'mon Jordan –let's go," Tyler said as they went inside the precinct.

"What happened Tyler?" Jordan asked.

"I need you to stay calm Jordan," Tyler answered.

"And I need you to tell me what happened Tyler," Jordan repeated. Tyler had that look of fear in his face again.

"Detective Rosa and Detective Morack followed Trenice to work today... they went into one of the hearing rooms... they started to question her... she tried to leave... and Detective Rosa wouldn't let her leave... Detective Morack grabbed her... threw her into the chair... she told Detective Barros her back was hurting... he took her to the hospital... called me... then I called you," Tyler answered. Jordan stood there for a few moments then went outside to talk to Jake.

"What's wrong man?" Jake asked as Jordan broke down.

"He put his fuckin' hands on my wife," Jordan answered.

"What?" Jake asked in shock.

"He put his fuckin' hands on my wife... He put his fuckin' hands on my wife... He put his fuckin' hands on my wife!" Jordan yelled as he slammed his fist into the dashboard.

"I got you," Jake said as he put his arm around Jordan.

"I know," Jordan said.

"He fucked with the wrong one... you're even more dangerous than I am," Jake said.

"Le'me get back inside," Jordan said.

"You won't have any more problems outta either one of those detectives," Detective Barros said as we came down the hall.

"Trenice..." Jordan whispered as he ran towards me, grabbed me into a tight hug, and picked me up off the floor. "Are you sure you're okay?"

"Yes Honey... but I can't breathe...," I laughed.

"Oh – sorry about that," Jordan laughed as he put me down.

"What did you do to Tyler? I've never seen him like that," I laughed.

"Why would I do anything to Tyler," Jordan laughed.

"I've never seen you like that Jordan," Tyler said.

"And as long as Trenice is okay, you'll never see me like that again," Jordan said.

"Good afternoon Mr. Williams," Detective Barros said. "May I speak with you in private?"

"Sure," Jordan answered as he motioned for Tyler to join them. Tyler was all too happy to oblige and I watched the three of them go into Detective Barros' office. As soon as the door closed, I got up and stood outside the door so I could hear what was being discussed.

"Mr. Williams, I saw what happened to your wife earlier this morning and I called your attorney so he could meet us down here to help your wife file a formal complaint," Detective Barros said.

"You called our attorney to help my wife file a complaint? Why would you do that?" Jordan asked.

"I understand your confusion," Detective Barros answered. "I called your attorney because you and your wife have been harassed by Detective Rosa and Detective Morack – and it needs to stop – today!" he yelled as he slammed his fist down on the table.

"As much as I agree with you – I'm a little leery," Jordan said.

"I understand completely," Detective Barros said. "Your wife has already filed the complaint and it's been signed off by me – hopefully this matter will be resolved and the next time your wife sees me it will be under more pleasant circumstances."

"Can I ask you a question?" Jordan asked.

"Sure," Detective Barros answered.

"What were you doing there?" Jordan asked.

"That's not your business," Detective Barros answered.

"Well excuse me," Jordan laughed.

"I'm sorry," Detective Barros said.

"That's okay," Jordan laughed.

"Can I help you?" the officer asked me before they came out of Detective Barros' office.

"No you can't," I answered.

"Who are you waiting for?" she asked.

"I'm sorry – who are you?" I asked.

"I'm Officer Rosa," she answered.

"Pleased to meet you," I said as I extended my hand. "I'm Trenice Williams."

"I can't talk to you," she answered as she turned to walk down the hall towards her husband. I could see them having a conversation as she pointed towards me and I bust out laughing.

"What's so funny?" Detective Barros asked as he, Jordan, and Tyler came out of his office.

"I just met Detective Rosa's wife," I laughed.

"She shouldn't be speaking to you," Detective Barros said.

"I know," I laughed. "She just told me."

"She just told you?" Detective Barros asked.

"Yes!" I laughed. "I was standing here, she asked me if she could help me, I asked her who she was, she told me her name, I said pleased to meet you – I'm Trenice Williams – I extended my hand, she told me she couldn't speak to me – and walked away!" At this point I was laughing so hard I was holding my stomach.

"Have a nice day," Detective Barros said as he went down the hall towards Detective Rosa and his wife, shaking his head.

"Let's get outta here," Tyler said as we followed him outside.

"I need to get back to the office," Tyler said. "My paralegal is already working on it – I'll give you a call sometime next week," he said as he jumped in his car and took off.

"What did you do to Tyler Man?" Jake laughed.

"I scared the shit outta him," Jordan answered.

"I'm talking y'all home – we need to talk," Jake said.

"I'm so done talking!" I said.

"You not speakin' to me? Really?" Jake laughed.

"Oh alright," I laughed as we got in the car.

Chapter 110

When we got to our building Carl met us in the lobby. "Hey y'all," he beamed. "I was hoping I'd see you before I got off work – I really need to talk to you."

"Hey Carl," Jake said.

"What time do you get off Carl?" Jordan asked.

"I get off in about 2 hours," he answered.

"Okay – why don't you come by when you get off work – and bring Char – then we can all hang out," Jordan said.

"Okay – I'll do that – I'ma call Char now," he said as he took out his phone and went back behind the concierge desk. When we got upstairs I couldn't wait to sit down and put my feet up.

"You sit there and relax Beautiful – I'll get you something to drink and when I come back, I'll rub your feet," Jordan said.

"Thank you Honey," Jake said.

"Call Rachel and tell her to come over so we can talk," I said.

"Okay – shoot – I left my phone downstairs in the car... le'me go get it," Jake said.

"Here – use my phone – then when she gets here she can get your phone out the car," I said as I handed him the phone. Jordan came into the living room with a tray of sweet ice tea but as soon as he saw my phone he dropped the tray, spilling ice tea and broken glass all over the floor.

"You aaight?" Jake asked as he jumped up from the couch and picked up the tray and the broken glass. Jordan just stood there, staring at me...

"Trenice?"

"Yes Honey?"

"Is this blood?" he asked as he picked up my cell phone.

"Yea," I answered. Jake came into the living room with paper towels and started cleaning up the sweet ice tea and glass off the floor...

"Oh my God... not again... I can't take this," Jordan said.

"What's wrong?" Jake asked as he got up off the floor.

"We need to go back to the hospital – she's bleeding!" Jordan yelled.

"Honey – I'm okay!" I said.

"No you're not – you're bleeding – we gotta get you to the hospital!" Jordan yelled.

"Honey – It's not my blood!" I yelled.

"Wait... what?" they both said in unison.

"It's not my blood," I repeated.

"You sure you're okay?" Jordan asked.

"Yes Honey – I'm fine," I said.

"Whose blood is it?" Jake asked.

"It's Detective Morack's blood," I answered.

"Wait... what?" they both said in unison.

"It's Detective Morack's blood," I repeated.

"How the hell did Detective Morack's blood get on your phone?" Jake asked as they both sat down.

"I bust him in the head with it," I answered.

"My girl!" Jake said as he pulled me into a hug.

"Wait... wait... wait – you bust Detective Morack's head open – he's bleeding – and you didn't get arrested?" Jordan asked.

"He tried to arrest me – he cuffed me – and Detective Rosa took my phone – then Detective Barros came into the hearing room and took the phone away from him and told Detective Morack to take the cuffs off me – but I backed away from him so Detective Barros took the cuffs off me himself," I answered, then I heard a knock at the door. "Who is it?" I asked.

"It's Rachel Trenice." I got up to open the door. As soon as she saw me, she knew something was wrong. "Come here girl," she said as she grabbed me into a hug. "What happened?"

"How much time do you have?" I laughed.

"Oh boy – let me sit down – here Babe," she said as she handed Jake his phone.

"How did you know Jake was here?" I asked.

"He called me to tell me you were in the hospital – where else would he be?" she answered.

"You're right," I laughed.

"So what happened?" she asked.

"The Detectives followed me to work and tried to trick me into getting arrested – but it backfired," I laughed.

"Wait... what?" she asked.

"They followed me to work. They started questioning me. I tried to leave – Detective Morack snatched me, threw me in the chair – I bust him upside his head with my phone – he tried to arrest me – but instead Detective Barros told him to get his ass downstairs so the Chief could come pick him up," I laughed.

"I don't believe this shit," she laughed.

"I told Detective Barros my back was hurting so he took me to the hospital to make sure I was okay before we went to the precinct to file a complaint," I said.

"Wait... wait... wait – Detective Barros knows you bust Detective Morack upside the head – he doesn't let you get arrested – he takes you to the hospital – then he helps you file a complaint? Somethin' ain't right," Rachel said.

"That's exactly what I said," Jordan said.

"This shit is crazy!" Rachel said.

"Detective Barros told me he knew we were being harassed by Detective Rosa and Detective Morack and he was putting a stop to it," Jordan said.

"Be careful with him," Rachel said.

"I already told him I didn't trust him," Jordan said.

"I didn't know you went through all that Trenice," Jake said.

"Yea – it's been a hell of a day," I said.

"Here," Jordan said as he handed me a glass of sweet ice tea, then went back into the kitchen.

"I thought you weren't going back to work yet," Rachel said.

"Here," Jordan said as he handed Rachel a glass of sweet ice tea, then went back into the kitchen.

"I'm not – I just went to drop off some papers," I said. Jordan came back into the living room, handed Jake a glass of sweet ice tea, placed one on the table for himself, sat down on the couch, lifted my feet into his lap, and then started massaging them.

"Oooohhh... that feels gooood," I moaned.

"You need us to leave?" Rachel laughed.

"No – stay and watch," I laughed.

"Your marriage started off with a bang!" Rachel laughed.

"Not a bang... a few kisses... oh wait – the headboard did hit the wall – I guess you could say a bang too," Jordan laughed.

"I'm pregnant," I said.

"Oh my God! Already? Congratulations!" Rachel said as she grabbed me into a hug. "Wait... is everything okay?"

"Yes – I'm fine, Araura's fine," I said as I handed her the picture of my sonogram.

"She's a cutie," Rachel said. "I didn't know you were so far along.

"How can you tell?" Jake asked.

"Here," Jordan said as he handed Jake the sonogram picture.

"Look at that! A lil' baby! I've never seen one of these before," Jake said.

"You ever gonna have children?" Jordan asked Jake.

"Maybe," Jake answered. Rachel smiled to herself.

"So who got your condo?" Jake asked.

"You wanna tell 'em Trenice?" Jordan asked.

"No I don't," I answered.

"Why not" it's not like we know them," Rachel laughed.

"So you got a better offer?" Jake asked.

"Yea," Jordan answered.

"Well – we tried," Jake said.

"You still lookin'?" Jordan asked.

"Hell yea – I love Mom but it's time to go! Jake laughed.

"Damn right it is" Rachel laughed.

"I'm surprised you lasted this long Rachel," Jordan laughed. "Jake's mom is no joke."

"Neither am I," Rachel laughed. "That's why we bump heads."

"They damn sure do – I have to admit though – you're the only woman I know that doesn't back down from my mother," Jake laughed.

"And I never will," Rachel laughed. "But I know deep down she loves me – that's why I put up with her.

"I thought you put up with her because you love me," Jake laughed.

"Yea… that too," Rachel laughed.

"Hello?" Jake said as he answered his phone. "Uh huh… okay… we'll meet you downstairs."

"Where are we going?" Rachel asked.

"We're meeting Vanessa on the 7th floor," Jake answered.

"We are?" Rachel asked.

"Yea – something just came on the market and she wants us to jump on it before someone else does," he said as he got up to head towards the door.

"Let's go," Jordan said as we all got up.

"You don't need to come with us – stay here with Trenice," Jake said.

"I wanna go," I said.

"Alrighty – let's go then," Jordan said as we all headed out the door.

"Where's everybody going?" Carl asked as the elevator door opened.

"We're going to the 7th floor," Jake answered as we all got in the elevator.

"Hi Char," I said. Char just looked at me. When we got to the 7th floor Vanessa bust out laughing.

"I didn't think we were having a family reunion so soon... follow me," she said as we went to the end of the hall. When she opened the door everyone smiled.

"Babe – it's so bright in here – I love it – can we take it? Please?" Rachel asked.

"You really want it?" Jake asked.

"Yes Babe," she answered.

"We'll take it Vanessa," Jake said.

"Don't you think you should see it first?" she asked.

"Yes I do – but it doesn't matter – we're still gonna take it," Jake said as he pulled Rachel into a kiss.

"I love you so much," Rachel said.

"I love you too," Jake said. "Let's see our new home," he said as he pulled Rachel close to him.

"It's nice and bright in here," Char said.

"Yes it is – this is a corner unit so you get sunlight from both sides," Vanessa said.

"This is a large master suite," Jake said. We all followed Vanessa down the hall towards the master suite.

"Oh this is nice," Carl said. "It doesn't look this big by the size of this condo.

"This would be perfect for us," Char said. Jordan and I looked at each other. Carl smiled to himself.

"What's that about?" Char asked.

"Nothing," I answered.

"Yea right," Char smirked.

"Hey Babe – this guest room is just right for my mom," Jake said.

"Your mom?" Rachel asked.

"Calm down Babe - I said guest room," he said as he kissed her.

"Okay – but as soon as we turn that room into a nursery your mom's outta luck," Rachel laughed.

"You got it," Jake said as he kissed her again.

"I love you," Rachel said.

"I love you more," Jake said.

"Oh dear," Vanessa said from the kitchen. We all went towards the kitchen. When we got there no one said anything. Rachel bust out laughing.

"You okay Babe?" Jake asked.

"Yes," she laughed.

"I'm sorry about the kitchen," Vanessa said. "This is one of the reason's he lowered the asking price. You still want it?"

"Yea," Rachel said.

"Thank God!" Vanessa said. "When you bust out laughing you had me worried.

"I wasn't worried – I know exactly why she's laughing," Jake said.

"Why is she laughing?" Vanessa asked.

"Because this kitchen looks exactly like my mother's kitchen," Jake answered. That did it...

"AAAAHHHHHHHH...
HA, HA, HA, HA, HA, HA, HA, HA, HA, HA, HA, HA, HA, HA, HA, HA, HA, HA, HA, HA... AAAAHHHHHHHHH...
HA, HA, HA, HA, HA, HA, HA, HA, HA, HA, HA, HA, HA, HA, HA, HA, HA, HA, HA, HA... AAAAHHHHHHHHH...
HA, HA, HA, HA, HA, HA, HA, HA, HA, HA, HA, HA, HA, HA, HA, HA, HA, HA, HA, HA... AAAAHHHHHHHHH...
HA, HA, HA, HA, HA, HA, HA, HA, HA, HA, HA, HA, HA, HA, HA, HA, HA, HA, HA... AAAAHHHHHHHHH...

HA, HA, HA, HA, HA, HA, HA, HA, HA, HA, HA, HA, HA, HA, HA, HA, HA, HA, HA, HA..."

"Let's go see the other bedroom," Vanessa said.

"Another bedroom? Where?" Carl asked.

"It's off the kitchen," Vanessa said.

"This is cute – a lil' small but cute," Carl said.

"It is cute," Rachel said. "I love the view of the trees from the window – this is my room," Rachel said.

"What are you going to do about the kitchen?" Vanessa asked.

"We can always update the kitchen," Rachel said.

"So you still want it then?" Vanessa asked.

"Yea – I still want it," Rachel said as she looked at Jake.

"Okay then – I'll get started on the paperwork right away – I want to get him this offer before his family tries to change his mind again," Vanessa said.

"Change his mind? They better not," Jake laughed.

"I really like this bathroom," we all heard Char say from the guest bathroom. When we got down the hall we all took turns going inside.

"It's very nice," Carl said.

"It's big," Jake laughed. "I'm surprised we all fit in here."

"I don't get it – he renovated everything but the kitchen," Jordan said.

"He saved that for me," Rachel said.

"I need to get back to the office – I'll talk to you soon – bye everybody!" Vanessa said as she locked the door and headed towards the elevator.

"So we're going back upstairs now?" Char asked.

"Yes we are," Carl said as he pulled Char into a kiss.

"Wow," Char said.

"Wow is right," Carl said as they got to the elevator before us.

"I can't believe we're going to live in this building – I always wanted to live here," Rachel said.

"You did Babe?" Jake asked.

"Yea," she answered.

"I never knew that," Jake said.

"You have a lot to learn," Rachel laughed as she pulled Jake into a kiss.

"Teach me," he said as he kissed her back. Carl and Char looked back at us and smiled. When we got to the 30th floor we got off the elevator and walked down the hall. No one said anything. Jordan opened the door, we all went into the living room, and sat down.

"Okay that's it – y'all are up to somethin' and I'm not leaving until I know what it is," Char said. We all bust out laughing.

"No one's up to anything Char – I promise," Carl said as he pulled her into a kiss.

"I don't know what you're up to – but I like it," Char said as she kissed him back.

"We might as well tell her, Jordan said.

"Okay – I'll tell her," I said.

"I know this is gonna be good," Char said.

"It is Char – I'm pregnant."

"You're pregnant?" Carl asked. "Oh my God – that's wonderful – congratulations!" Carl said as he pulled me into a hug.

"Thanks Carl," I laughed.

"I'm so happy for you Trenice," Char said as she hugged me.

"Show 'em the pictures," Rachel said.

"You got pictures? Already? Le'me see!" Char said.

"Oh look at the tiny baby!" Carl said. "God bless y'all!"

"Amen!" Jordan and I said in unison.

"You're about two months right?" Char asked.

"Yea Char," I answered.

"When did you find out you were pregnant?" Char asked.

"Right before the wedding," I answered.

"So you found out on your wedding day?" Char asked.

"Yea," I answered.

"What's her name?" Char asked.

"Her name is Araura," Jordan answered.

"That's a beautiful name," Carl said.

"Thanks Carl," Jordan said.

"This sonogram has today's date on it," Char said.

"Yes it does," I said.

"So you got it today?"

"Yes I did."

"It says White Plains Hospital."

"Yes it does," I laughed.

"I'll take that," Jordan laughed as he extended his hand to take the picture. "I'm going to put these away," Jordan said as he went towards the bedroom.

"So why did you go to White Plains Hospital?" Char asked.

"My back started bothering me so I went to the hospital before I came home," I answered.

"I'm surprised you didn't go to your own doctor."

"I did go to my own doctor."

"I thought your doctor was in Yonkers."

"She is in Yonkers."

"Are you done Detective?" Carl asked. We all bust out laughing.

"Yea, I'm done," Char laughed.

"Good – now we can get down to business," Jordan said.

"Business?" Char asked.

"We put our condo on the market," Jordan said.

"You did?" Char asked.

"Yes we did – and we got an offer on it," Jordan said.

"Already? That was fast," Char said.

"Yes it was," Jordan said. "We got the offer on Sunday.

"Wow – somebody really wanted your condo," Char said. "I wonder who it was?"

"It was me," Carl answered.

"You?" Char, Jake, and Rachel asked in unison.

"Yes my love," Carl answered as he took Char's hand. "I bought it for us," he said as he pulled her into a kiss."

"I love you Carl," Char said as she started to cry.

"I love you too Char," Carl said as he started crying.

"Where's that damn basket at?" Jake asked as we all laughed.

Chapter 111

"Who is it?" I yawned.

"It's Tyler," Jordan yawned as he answered the phone and put it on speaker.

"Good morning Tyler," I yawned.

"Good morning Trenice," Tyler said. "Sorry to wake you so early – I just wanted you to know the paperwork's been filed and you'll be getting a court date soon."

"She shouldn't even have to go to court," Jordan said.

"Good morning Jordan," Tyler said.

"Good morning Tyler," Jordan said.

"I'll let you get back to whatever you were doing," Tyler laughed.

"What – no coffee?" Jordan laughed.

"Are you inviting me over for coffee?" Tyler asked.

"Sure Tyler – c'mon over," Jordan said.

"I wish I could – but I've got a full calendar today," Tyler said.

"Maybe next time," Jordan said.

"Maybe," Tyler said.

"Have a good day Tyler," I said.

"You too Trenice, Jordan," Tyler said as he hung up.

"What shall we do now Beautiful?" Jordan asked as he came up behind me, pulled me into a hug, and started kissing me on the back of my neck...

"Mmmm... we could do some more of this," I said as turned around to face Jordan and pulled him into a kiss.

"Let's take this into the bedroom," Jordan said between kisses.

"Okay...," I breathed as we continued kissing and walking towards the bedroom.

"Who's calling now?" I asked between kisses.

"Hold that thought," Jordan said as he stopped kissing me to answer the phone. "Hello? Now? Okay – I'll be right there," he said as he hung up.

"Where are you going Honey?" I asked.

"I gotto go – something happened at work – I'll be back as soon as I can, he said as he grabbed his jacket.

"Okay – I'm going back to bed Honey – I'll see you later – I hope everything's okay at work," I yawned before I kissed him goodbye.

"See you soon Beautiful," Jordan said, then kissed me goodbye. "I'll wake you when I get back," he said as we continued kissing.

"If you don't get outta here I'm taking you back to bed," I said.

"Okay – see you soon," he said as he headed towards the door, stopped to pick up my cell phone, then left. When he got in the elevator, he went to my videos, played the video I recorded... and got really angry.

Detective Barros knew Jordan wasn't in a good place when he saw him. "He put his hands on my wife," Jordan said.

"I had nothing to do with that."

"You said you would make sure Trenice didn't get hurt... you promised... and you broke that promise," Jordan said as he started to play the video I recorded.

"I know about that – I already have it," Detective Barros said.

"Listen to it again," Jordan said as he stepped closer.

"I did everything I could," Detective Barros said.

"You're not telling me what I want to hear," Jordan said.

"You don't understand," Detective Barros said.

"I understand perfectly," Jordan said. "You're the one who doesn't understand. He put his hands on my wife – now you have another problem – and you need to take care of it… before I do," Jordan said.

"I can't do that," Detective Barros said.

"You can take care of him just like you took care of what happened in the parking lot," Jordan said.

"You don't have to threaten me," Detective Barros said. "I get it."

"Glad to hear it," Jordan said. Detective Barros walked away from Jordan, got in his car, and drove off. Jordan headed towards the newsstand and went inside.

"Mr. Jordan – how are you?" the cashier said behind the counter.

"I'm good – and hungry," Jordan laughed.

"Two specials: one with grits and shrimp – one with home fries – turkey sausage – one white toast – one whiskey down," the cashier told the cook. "Let me get your coffee for you," he said as he made the coffee. When the breakfast was ready the cashier bagged everything up and Jordan handed him $5. "Have a great day Mr. Jordan," the cashier said.

"Thank you – you too," Jordan said as he went outside... and ran right into Detective Morack.

"Watch where the fuck you're going!" Detective Morack said. Jordan stood there in the doorway and looked Detective Morack directly in his eyes without moving. "Get the fuck outta my way!" Detective Morack yelled.

"Make me," Jordan said.

"I can arrest you," Detective Morack said.

"A man dressed in plain clothes who isn't an officer because he's been suspended can't do shit," Jordan laughed.

"What did you say?" Detective Morack asked.

"I said you ain't shit and you can't do shit," Jordan laughed.

"That's not what your wife said the other day," Detective Morack said. "She sure felt good in my arms," Detective Morack said as he went back towards his car. Jordan followed right behind him.

"Are you still married Detective?" Jordan asked.

"Yes I am – why?"

"Glad to hear it."

"What's that supposed to mean?"

"They'll need to notify your next of kin."

"What the hell are you talking about?"

"Your funeral," Jordan answered as he flagged down a cab, got in, and took off. When

Jordan got back home, he placed my phone on the table, took the breakfast out the bag, placed it on the tray, and then came into the bedroom to wake me up.

"Mmmm... you're back already," I said between kisses as the aroma from the food and coffee teased my nose.

"I got breakfast," he said as he started getting undressed.

"I see," I said as he picked up the tray, brought it over to the bed, and climbed in beside me. "Oooohhh... you went to our favorite spot in Getty Square," I said as I started drinking my coffee.

"The best $5 you'll ever spend," Jordan said as he sipped his tea, turned on News 12, and we listened to Jeanine Rose state the following:

"We interrupt our regularly scheduled program to bring you this latest news. Detective Morack of the Yonkers Police Department has died. According to witnesses, Detective Morack collapsed in Getty Square earlier this morning after stopping to pick up his breakfast from the newsstand. Reports indicate he suffered a massive heart attack and was pronounced dead upon arrival at St. Joseph's Hospital. No other details are being released at this time. We now return to our regularly scheduled programming."

"Well... at least I don't have to face him in court," I said as I continued drinking my coffee..."

"No you don't Beautiful," Jordan said as he finished his tea, put the cup down, turned off the television, placed the tray in our lap, and we finished breakfast.

Group Discussion Questions

1. What is the one **'Secret'** that Jordan, Trenice, Char, Jake, Rachel, Dr. Campton, and Dr. Campton's nurse will carry to their graves?

2. How did Thomas become one of the major characters in the series? How was he brought back from the dead?

3. How did News 12 become a major character in the story?

4. What was the significance of the pot hole? Why was it so important?

5. Who killed Dr. Aiden?

6. Is Trudy dead? If so, who killed her?

Answer Key

Question 1: Trenice killed her rapist.

Question 2:

Thomas slept with Miss Gladys and her daughter, Claire, Thomas is Trudy and Trenice's father, Thomas is Cornell's father (which means Trenice was raped by her own brother) and Thomas is Tony's father. Thomas was brought back from the dead by News 12.

Question 3:

a. News 12 was on the scene when the Gas Station blew up.

b. News 12 was also on the scene when friends gathered at Ceratto Park to grieve Cornell.

c. News 12 was on the scene at Brooks Funeral Home when fights broke out.

d. News 12 identified the 2nd person in the explosion as Thomas Johnson.

Answer Key

e. News 12 identified Cornell Jones as Thomas's son.

f. News 12 reported Dr. Aiden's arrest.

g. News 12 reported Dr. Aiden's murder.

h. News 12 reported Detective Morack's death.

Question 4:

Trenice thanked God for creating the pot hole because it slowed down the ambulance so she could get inside. This also provided an explanation for why pot holes exist.

www.ingramcontent.com/pod-product-compliance
Lightning Source LLC
Chambersburg PA
CBHW062128170626
46813CB00002B/607